PHILIP STEVENS

THE BUTTERFLY
&
THE BOOT

THE BUTTERFLY
&
THE BOOT

The Butterfly & The Boot

A 'coming of age' story set during the period of 1958 to 1974. Three naturally interwoven lives develop against an influential backdrop of nurture and social history with an enduring musical thread.

About the Author

Philip Stevens grew up in Norwich during the period covered by this story.

Whilst all characters and situations are fictitious, they do reflect the observations and influences of the author during that formative period of his early life.

The author's love, and appreciation, of family, true friends, music and football hopefully shine through.

With thanks to Simonne Kaye for help in getting this project over the final hurdle and to Katy Atzberger for her proof-reading skills.

"The story is dedicated to my wife and in memory of my good buddy PA."

Philip Stevens 2019.

'If I had one light that I could shine on you,
I would shine it on your very soul just to see you through.
Though I don't have a light, I do have a soul,
Only my soul is for you.'

Free 1971.

Table of Contents

(Intentionally blank)

Chapter 1 ~ 1960

The wasp landed and stung its victim immediately.

Jake, as always, reacted violently and struck the striped creature with the back of his stocky, seven-year-old hand. The blow sent the intruder spiralling through the air. It crash-landed on the concrete playground, momentarily twitching before it died. Jake grinned as he sucked at his reddening forearm.

On the opposite side of the playground of Saint John's infant school, two other seven year olds were observing a butterfly perform its natural dance. It hovered and darted as the splendour of its colours enraptured the two observers, who gaped in silent unison at the beauty of this creature.

Will was crouched on his haunches, with his mouth wide open at the wonder before him. Mary was on her knees beside him, their heads touching as they watched, completely entranced. They stared in fixed amazement as the apparently random, controlled movements finally ended in settlement on the grass in front of them.

The 'Red Admiral' displayed the majestic beauty of its symmetrically, kaleidoscopic wings, before bringing them together as it reached a temporary resting place. The two children looked at each other and smiled longingly as the object of their pleasure finally settled.

From nowhere a booted foot viciously parted them and crashed down on the subject of their joint gaze.

The butterfly was crushed and died instantly.

Jake grinned again as he lifted his foot, knocking Will to the ground in the process. Mary screamed and ran away, her long dark hair bounced on the back of her blue school cardigan and tears poured from her brown eyes.

Playtime was over.

Jake ambled arrogantly back to the school buildings, walking straight through a game of 'ciggies' being played against the school wall and simultaneously sending the playing cards everywhere. A momentary squeal of protest from one of the players was met by the 'Jake stare'.

The protest ended immediately.

Will remained unmoved from his position, where he had been unceremoniously dumped, staring with disbelief at the innocent crushed creature. The colours were still the same: red, black and white but the beauty was now trapped in lifelessness.

Will recovered his position, moved the blond fringe from his eyes and sneakily wiped a tear trickle from his cheek. He carefully peeled the butterfly from its cold, concrete coffin and laid it between two pages of his reading book.

It nestled comfortably between 'Janet and John'.

He placed the book slowly into his satchel and went to join the others in the queue at the school entrance. The queue moved slowly as the teacher dispensed the daily dose of cod liver oil into each gaping mouth in turn. Will, as usual, flushed the disgusting taste away with a cup of orange juice and went to find Mary in the classroom. He took the seat at the desk next to her.

Jake merely grinned from the back of the room.

Chapter 2 ~ 1958

Jake slid under the bedclothes as it begun. The noise, as usual, had woken him.

'Where's my bleedin' dinner,' screamed Joe Kirke at his cowering wife. She knew what was coming.

'It's in the bleedin' dog!' she bravely responded, and immediately winced as he raised his large, hairy fist and aimed it in her direction.

She turned as he struck, catching her on the weak spot just above her left eye. She fell, crashing against the chair and landed on the floor. Blood poured from where he had made contact. Joe kicked her in the midriff while she lay there clutching at her eye.

He was a real man.

He grinned as he looked at her, 'Not so bleedin' funny now is it?'

The crash of the chair and the screams of his mother frightened Jake and he crept further down the bed, but through the uncarpeted floorboards of his bedroom he couldn't avoid hearing everything going on below.

'Get my bleedin' dinner on this table NOW, you

bleedin' cow!' slurred Joe, 'I'm going for a piss and get me another bleedin' beer.'

When he returned, she had done all he had demanded and was, at the same time, trying to stem the flow of blood with a tea towel.

'What've you done now, you stupid bitch?'

'I tripped and fell,' she lied. He knew no different in his drunken state. He sat down, slurped his beer, belched immediately and began to stuff himself. 'I'll have another beer and then you can piss off to bed!' he spouted.

Jake absorbed it all, although he tried to shut out the sounds with sleep. Joe hadn't always been like this.

In fact, in the beginning it was instant love for the young Jenny Bryce. He was a bit of a catch with his dark wavy hair and those eyes. Of course, once she fell with the baby, they had had to get married.

This was the start of their troubles. Joe didn't take fatherhood and marriage seriously and preferred the public house to going home. His 'mates' were still fancy free, and their life seemed a million miles from his. They were never greeted with a 'What time do you call this?' or 'Where have you been?' And, although they all worked in the same factory, doing the same boring job for 9 hours a day, Joe's lot always seemed a much bigger burden than the one they carried.

The days passed slowly, the frustrations appeared greater for him as his pay packet had to be shared. Then of course there was 'Brownie'. The factory manager, John Brown, always seemed to pick on Joe. According to Joe, Brownie was a 'bleedin', pompous, poofed up pillock' (Jake had heard that phrase a thousand times) who lived on that posh estate and did nothing but sit behind a desk and dish out the orders.

Joe Kirke and John Brown never saw eye to eye. The final crunch came when Joshua arrived at the factory. Brownie, knowing full well that Joe had an inherent hatred of blacks, or 'wogs' as Joe affectionately called them, put the two of them next to each other on the production line. And worse asked, no told, Joe to look after him!

Joshua Jones (soon nicknamed JJ) had just arrived from the Caribbean with hundreds of his fellow countrymen and was eager to learn and please.

He never stood a chance. Joe made his life hell.

'You're bleedin' useless, jump on the bleedin' 'Banana Boat' and go back to where you came from!' was one of his politer comments. The origin of Joe's hatred was a mystery, but the seeds were probably planted by ignorance and fear a long time ago. It didn't matter how or when, it simply meant that JJ suffered.

So too did Jenny Kirke.

The only time Joe could accept his lot was when he was drunk. He went with the 'lads' every Friday and Saturday to the 'King's Head'. There he was the life and soul of the party. He bought drinks and he drunk. He was bought drinks and he drunk. He sang and he drunk. He laughed and he drunk. He got drunk.

As usual, at the end of the night, when 'last orders' was called, 10.50pm on the dot, he'd want 'one for the road'. His so-called mates then began the ritual of herding him out of the pub and escorting him home. It was a slow, supportive walk through the estate where they all lived.

At number 52 Churchill Road, they stopped, took him up the path, opened the door and shoved him in.

He picked himself up, staggered in and went to find his punch bag. Jake was the future consequence of his actions.

Chapter 3

'The Rise' was a private estate which had been established well before the 'new' council estate was started in 1950: It was home to the Browns.

'Mile End' was to be 'the new beginning for the working man' and designed to sweep away the post-war housing/lifestyle depression, providing a country-like 'residence' within striking distance of Town. Or so the Council's declarations boldly declared.

It had been built under the directive of the day to provide affordable accommodation (rented) for the working class. Mile End was built as a self-contained site with a structured array of well- built houses, each with an ample garden.

The proximity of shops, transport, and schools were all part of the post-war plan to keep the tenants happy.

The 'King's Head' helped too.

A nearby industrial park provided the jobs, the largest employer being 'Brown's Boxes' which laboriously churned out cardboard boxes in their thousands every day.

The idea of such an estate was, in theory, an affordable, better option for many working people and there was soon a waiting list.

The biggest problem for the estate was some of those people.

John Brown had always been philosophical about the new council estate; in particular it meant he had a ready supply of workers for his cardboard factory.

John had taken over the day to day running of the factory, in time honoured tradition, from his Father, having joined the business straight from University. He had studied Engineering and to his Father's delight had gained a First-Class Honours degree.

To John this was a secondary result of his three years at Brunel. The real 'First' was that it was there that he had met the only love of his life: Margaret or, as he had always known and loved her, Mags. Margaret's passion, since childhood, was reading and it came as no surprise that she eventually went on to university to study English Literature.

Life's unravelling tapestry demanded that they went to the same place. It was in the library that they met:

Margaret was there, studying as usual, and had just got up from her desk to leave, with her clutch of books, when this loud, intrusive 'whirlwind' arrived.

Four strapping, mud-encrusted young men entered, throwing a rugby ball to each other across the hitherto, silent library. They were completely and inebrietly oblivious to the fact that they were no longer on the playing field!

Bizarre!

The whole library stared in open-mouthed shock.

The thrown ball smacked Margaret straight in the head and knocked her sideways spilling her books all across the floor. The library room silence returned as the 'whirlwind' came to an abrupt end.

Three of the unwelcome intruders made a sharp, exit leaving John to 'sort it out'. A somewhat slurred, whispered apology exited his mouth as he bent down towards her as she lay on the floor. She was shocked, not hurt. She looked up. He looked down.

It was truly love at first sight

'What the hell do you think you are doing?' she screamed at him. She was greeted by a congregational 'Shh!'

'Sorry,' was all he could reply, trying to stifle a laugh he could sense building up inside.

She tried to look serious, but he looked so out of place with his mud splattered face peering down at her through that mop of dark, dishevelled hair. His black and gold rugby shirt was torn, she noticed, and his thighs were enormous. He went to pick her up and she immediately responded, 'Don't even think of putting those disgusting looking hands anywhere near me!'

Then it happened.

Simultaneously they looked at each other and burst into spontaneous laughter. The absurdity of the moment struck home, as the usual 'Shh!' rained down on them, triggering even more laughter from the love-struck duo. This time he engulfed her in his arms and carried her to where laughter was permitted

They laughed and loved for their three years together and married in the spring of 1948.

Together they now shared their comfortable lifestyle with the three children they both idolised. They had always tried to instil true family values into their children and to encourage each of them to appreciate the privileges on offer.

Their family motto was 'you get precisely what you work for'.

James, the eldest, was born ten months after they were married and was a carbon copy of his Dad. There was no doubt he would achieve anything he wanted to in life, but he was already destined to, one day, run the family business.

The twins were unplanned but adored none the less. William was the youngest of the two by twenty minutes. His older, as she frequently reminded him, sister Susan was a carbon copy of William. Blonde and blue eyed. They were as one in everything and Susan looked after Will.

Only his Mother called him William. Maybe it was because she really preferred 'Margaret', to the contraction of a name her future husband had forever labelled her with on that first date after the famous library scrum down!

Chapter 4

Carol Rodgers was as settled as she had been for a long time. She could support her two girls and the house felt like home. The job in 'The Sweet Shop' was perfect as Mr. Smith allowed her to work around the children, although his unwelcome hands were often around her. She did nothing to encourage him and always laughed him off.

He was a widower of some years' experience. She had a lot to learn.

The two girls, Mary and Lizzie, were no trouble at all, as Mary was now settled at St John's infant school and Lizzie spent most days with her Nanny Wilson.

Her life shouldn't have turned out like this:

Carol and Roy were so happy when she learned that they were to have a second baby.

'A brother or sister for you,' she excitedly told Mary, who was just about old enough to understand.

Roy was so delighted he cracked open that bottle of sherry they had left over from Mary's christening. Neither of them finished their drink.

'I've been to see the council about getting one of the

houses on 'Mile End',' he told his smiling wife as he poured the remainder of the bottle down the sink.

'I only have to sign some papers and we should go straight to the top of the list, what with a second on the way.' She immediately hugged him, and Mary joined in, grabbing them both just below their respective knees, to make it a 'three-way cuddle'.

'Our very own house,' Carol squealed excitedly, 'With our very own family in it,' replied Roy. Roy never saw the house or his family in it.

After they had married, they, as many couples did then, had moved in with parents. Fortunately, Carol's mother, Jeanie Wilson, had plenty of space for the newlyweds as she had been left a widow after the war. Even when Mary arrived in March 1953, the house couldn't have been happier during those few years.

Roy awoke early that Thursday morning; he had a busy day ahead. Carol, as usual, was up as well to pack his lunch. He patted her growing bump and kissed her affectionately on the lips. He looked at her lovingly and produced that smile which seemed to fill his face and the one she had noticed from their first encounter.

She never saw that smile again.

Roy had been given permission to leave work early that day as he had an important meeting with Mr. Johnson of the Housing Department at the Town Hall. Mr. Johnson was an amiable man and he shared Roy's delight at the good news, they could move into their new dream home immediately.

It was a three bed-roomed house, no.56 Churchill Road, Mile End. It had a large garden which would be ideal for Mary, and her soon- to-arrive sibling, to play in. Roy was so excited when he left Mr. Johnson's office after signing the paperwork. He could hardly wait to get home to tell his family the news.

He never saw the bus coming.

'It would have been instantaneous,' the police officer told Mrs. Wilson as she sat in in her front room. 'He wouldn't have felt a thing,' he continued.

Carol was inconsolable as Mary, not really understanding where Daddy had gone, clung on to Mum.

'Did we swap our dad for a house?' she might have asked, if she could.

Carol was nothing if not determined. She was still going to move into their dream house, and she was going to make it work. It had been hard, but three years later she could see light at the end of the tunnel.

She missed him every day. He had been her friend, her lover, her shoulder to cry on, her rock and her life. He was the other half of their children. He gave so much love to Mary (his Princess) that she sometimes felt a guilty jealousy.

Mary's face told the full story whenever he had appeared. He would have shared his love with Lizzie, born four months after they laid Roy to rest.

She must go on for the girls and his memory.

Chapter 5

The mums had become friends by accident.

'The Park' on Mile End had been established by the caring council as a leisure facility and provided somewhere for all to go. It was actually named after some local dignitary, but everyone called it 'The Park'. The three mums went for their own reasons but, through the children, soon found friendship and a common cause.

For Carol it was her day off, the shop closed on Thursday afternoon and she could take the now toddling Lizzie together with Mary for 'some fresh air'. Jenny was always pleased to escape from her life and Jake needed to let out his frustrations.

He was getting hard to deal with and she couldn't wait for next year when the school could have the pleasure of his company. Mags always felt she was intruding, after all 'The Park' was on the estate.

'Do you think we should use it?'

'Don't be daft darling,' John had replied. 'It's paid for by tax payers, and I'm certainly one of them!'

Still she felt some trepidation the first time she

crossed the road to 'The Park'. The twins in tow she made her entrance. The bond was instantaneous, as Mary ran to the new arrivals and immediately grabbed the hands of Will and Susan and took them to see the ducks on the council pond.

She gripped Will's hand more tightly than Susan's. Jake sauntered along with them, pretending not to notice the new arrivals, and threw a stone at the first duck he saw.

'Why did you do that?' innocently and simultaneously inquired Susan and Will. 'Hate ducks and I don't like you two,' snarled Jake.

Susan cried. Will didn't, as he was distracted by Mary's grip. She still held his hand, although she had long since let go of Susan's.

'Look at that funny, beautiful butterfly,' she said pointing across the water. 'It's not a butterfly,' corrected Will 'It's a dragonfly, but it is beautiful.'

Will was obsessed with all thing's insect. His Dad had called it entomology or something, but he couldn't remember, or even pronounce such a big word.

He loved it all the same.

They were lost in their own world. Jake felt unwanted and so he sneakily pulled Susan's hair, she screamed and ran to her mother.

'Whatever is the matter?'

'That horrible boy pulled my hair,' she shrieked.

Not wanting to upset her newly found friends, who had immediately made her feel welcome, Mags quickly made an excuse for him and suggested that Susan went and played with Lizzie in the sand pit. Susan loved the responsibility and soon forgot about Jake.

The meetings in the park turned into a routine and the three mums became good friends. The ritual was always the same with Susan taking charge of Lizzie, who adored her new, younger 'Mum'. Will and Mary would spend hours looking, searching, prodding and digging around for anything of interest.

Jake was always there. Will tolerated him because Mary wouldn't allow otherwise.

Whenever he got up to his tricks, she always defended him,

'He didn't mean it ', and she would make those puppy dog eyes at Will, who would melt, forget whatever Jake had done, and agree.

Chapter 6 ~ 1959

And finally, the big day arrived.

Will was up and about first, he was so excited, 'Is it time yet?' he constantly asked his Mother. 'No William, soon.'

Susan was as excited, inside, but as usual she took it all in her stride and carried on playing with her doll. John and Mags had always made learning fun and the twins were more than prepared for St John's infant school, in fact they were more than ready for the local junior school. But, of course, they had to follow the system.

'When can we leave?' asked Will.

'At 8.30 William,' came the immediate response from his Mum.

John was just about ready to leave for work and as usual kissed them all except James who, at the age of ten, simply got a 'manly' touch on the head. James was already a star pupil and another product of the 'Browns' academy of home teaching'. He tolerated the twins but considered them an intrusion. He returned to his book and ignored Will's constant questioning.

'I bet Mary has already left,' Will quietly muttered. Nobody heard, or at least they all pretended not to.

John had wanted his offspring to opt out of state education and was more than willing to sacrifice part of their lifestyle to give them the advantages of private education.

It had started the only serious row of their married life.

Mags was adamant that the state system, with all its inherent faults, would provide the children with a proper all- round education, as it had for her and John. He, however, wanted to fast- track them to the top of the academic world to give them the best start in life. As usual they discussed every angle and, as usual, they compromised.

The deal was that the children (never referred to as kids) would all go to the local infant school and after the '11+' they would consider private schools. James had sat his '11+' early and was now attending 'Wilberforce College'.

The college only took the best and they started their route to excellence at ten years old. Wilberforce College was just a ten-minute drive from 'The Rise' and John had no problems dropping James off there every morning on his way to work.

'Got your rugby kit?' he asked James, knowing full well that it would have been packed the night before, as well as him having completed any homework for the next day. James wanted to be the best at whatever he did, sport was no exception.

'Packed and ready to go Dad,' he replied. He was a

'chip off the old block'.

They each kissed Mum and Mags respectively, waved to Susan, still getting her doll up, and passed Will standing in the hall ready to leave at 8am!

'Good luck today, William,' John said to his youngest son as he patted him in 'James' fashion on the head.

Will ducked out of the way, after all this was new to him, he usually got a kiss! 'When are we going?' he asked his Dad as the front door was opened.

'Soon son, try to be patient.' James completely ignored his tiresome brother and carried on reading his book as he followed his Father to the car, parked outside in the large drive.

'Right,' said Mother at 8.30 on the dot, to William and Susan 'Let's go.'

'Yes!' shrieked William as his clenched fist and bent arm prodded downwards. 'Ok Mum,' said Susan, calmly placing her doll against the cushion on the settee. The walk to the school would only take fifteen minutes.

After crossing the road from 'The Rise', they would pass through the park, along by the pond and straight to the school entrance. Will, of course, wanted to spend time by the pond but:

'Not today William,' was the immediate answer to his anticipated question. They arrived at the same time as the others.

Chapter 7

'When am I getting my bleedin' breakfast?' Joe demanded. 'You'll have to sort yourself out today,' answered Jenny. 'What's so bleedin' special about today?'

He didn't have clue.

'Only Jake's first day at school,' she answered, 'and he's very worried'.

'Waste of bleedin' time, if you ask me, he'll only end up in the bleedin' factory with me!' 'Well good job no one's asking you then!' she bravely replied. Joe was never violent when sober, and at breakfast he was usually, just about, alcohol free.

Jake emerged from the toilet for the third time that morning.

'I don't feel very well,' he pathetically mumbled as he held his stomach. 'I've got a tummy ache'.

'It's only first day nerves,' his mum tried to reassure him. 'You'll be alright when you see Mary, Will and Susan. '

'Are the kids of that bleedin', pompous, poofed up pillock going to our bleedin' school?' enquired Joe.

'It's not our school, it's for all who want to go there, and stop using that language in front of Jake.'

'What bleedin' language?' he, without having a clue, replied.

'Why can't Brownie send 'em to that posh place where his other bleedin' kid goes!' 'Cos they can't go there till they are ten,' she countered.

'And he pays tax like we do and can send his children where he chooses. Now here's your lunchbox so get away or you'll be late for work.'

'Who bleedin' cares!' he replied putting the plastic box of sandwiches into his haversack. The door slammed behind him.

'My tummy still hurts,' pathetically declared Jake, hoping now that his Dad had gone his Mum would relent and allow him to give the whole school 'thing' a miss.

She put her arm around him and gently rubbed his 'poorly' tummy. She noticed it was bulging more than a six-year old's should.

A potential 'chip off the old block' she sadly thought.

'There, there.' she calmly said, 'As soon as you see Mary, you'll be fine.'

During all those park meetings Mary, of all the children, was the one who always came to Jake's rescue when the others seemed to gang up on him after some incident.

Jenny never saw, or wanted to see, the reason for the 'incident '.

But she was right about Mary and knew that the

mention of her name would ease his 'aching' tummy.

'Right, let's get ready,' she gently whispered, as she removed her comforting arm from around Jake's shoulder and ceased the rotating motion of her hand on his midriff. Jake grudgingly smiled, as he knew he was beaten, and yes, he would be going to school today.

They packed his bag and left the house just after 8.30. They only had a short walk from Churchill Road, round the edge of the park and they would be at the entrance.

Chapter 8

'Lizzie, please let Mary get ready, we have to leave soon.'

Lizzie didn't realise yet that there was anything special about today. She just thought that Mum would go off to her sweet shop as usual and Nannie Wilson would look after her and her big sister.

Mr. Smith had, however, allowed Carol to take the day off so she could take Mary to school for her first day, and to be able to pick her up at the end.

Also, as Carol explained, 'Just in case.' She would probably have to allow him a couple of quick gropes, but it would be worth it to see Mary's face when she emerged from St John's infant school at the end of that day.

'I hope Jake is ok this morning,' Mary stated, with genuine concern showing on her young face.

'Why shouldn't he be?' queried her Mum.

'Well you know what he's like, but I bet Will was up and ready early.' She knew both characters so well.

'Where are we going, Mummy?' Lizzie asked, she was beginning to see that today's preparations were different.

Her Mum picked her up and explained that today was Mary's first day at school

'What's school?' she innocently asked, 'Can I go?' she continued before her Mum could explain.

'I'll be good, really.'

'You will go soon,' her Mum said while packing Mary's bag. 'When?' came the inevitable question.

The question and answer session went on for several returns until Carol reminded her youngest daughter that Nannie Wilson would soon be here to look after her, 'And only you!' she stressed. This brought a respite to the questioning as Lizzie considered the repercussions of this latest piece of information.

Meanwhile, Mary contemplated what the day might bring: She was apprehensive and ever so slightly worried, but she knew that Jake would be extremely worried, and it was her job to look out for Jake. She also knew that, for the first time in her life, she would spend the whole day with Will. She smiled inwardly at the thought and couldn't wait to see him.

Carol had always tried to encourage Mary to learn. But with Lizzie, the house, a full-time job and all the problems of a single mum she sometimes struggled to find the time to spend with Mary. They invariably found the only spare time was when Lizzie had finally gone to sleep, and they could snuggle up in bed and read together. Mary was 'a willing learner and she always tries hard', became Carol's assessment of her ability, which were comments to be repeated many times in Mary's future school reports.

Mary was caring and average.

Jeanie Wilson arrived on cue with the 'bribe' in her bag which Carol had agreed she could give to Lizzie, but only as a one off.

Lizzie ran excitedly to her Nan, jumping up as Jeanie's arms outstretched and landing against her chest as Nan planted a kiss on her youngest granddaughter's cheek and held her tightly.

'Have you got anything in your bag?' was Lizzie's standard question, which usually got a negative reply; but not today.

Lizzie ran off to play with her new doll as Nan went over to Mary.

The Nan and granddaughter, as always, hugged and kissed. Jeanie thought that Mary had the most beautiful smile she had ever seen and would do anything for her. Jeannie Wilson had been there every day since that dreadful day, two years ago, when Roy had died.

She was there first for Carol and Mary, then for Lizzie, born soon afterwards. She had so much admiration for her own daughter who was determined to bring up the girls as Roy would have wanted her to.

He would have wanted them to be respectful and mannered. He would have wanted them to be encouraged to always do their best, even if it wasn't the best. He would have wanted them to seek 'one fact more' before judging anyone or anything. He would have wanted them to see the best in everybody. Carol was doing all she could to achieve those aims.

Jeanie was, throughout it all, a 'wonderwall'.

'I'll keep Lizzie occupied while you and Mary get

going,' said Jeannie.

'Thanks, Mum,' replied Carol 'for everything' she added as a tear trickled down her cheek. Carol put on her own cardigan and then helped Mary into her new blue, school one.

They left the house and headed for the park. They continued on toward the school entrance and arrived almost at the same time as Will, Susan and Jake.

Will's eyes lit up when his soul mate arrived. Jake, also, suddenly relaxed and stopped scuffing his shoes along the ground. He had already been 'told off' by his mum for barging into Will. Will ignored Jake and after smiling at Mary continued staring at the school gates for whatever happened next.

Mrs Benson, Deputy Headmistress, happened next. She clapped loudly and everyone stopped whatever they were doing.

'Please Mums, bring your children into the school.'

Their new routine had begun. Will was first to the door as Jake grabbed Mary's hand and Susan brought up the rear.

Chapter 9 ~ 1966

It was the last day of term on a warm, balmy evening as the whole country was gripped by World Cup fever.

Will, as he did every day, left The King Edward Grammar school and crossed the road to enter the park opposite. He would dream his way through his ambling walk on the way to The Alderman John secondary school where Mary would be waiting for him. His satchel was strapped around his shoulder, filled with his desk contents. His uniform was looking the worse for wear at the end of his second year at grammar school.

Will had, as expected, sailed through the eleven plus and gone on to the next stage of his university preparation. He hadn't wanted to join his brother at the more exclusive, not to mention more expensive, Wilberforce College, but wanted instead to go to the nearer King Edward. His parents reluctantly agreed, although they would have been happy to make sacrifices to pay anything for his education.

Susan had also chosen to go to the local state grammar for girls, which actually backed onto the King Edward. The St John's Grammar school for girls was well established and its position meant that there was a close relationship between the two schools and Will never felt that he was too far from his twin. His main regret was that he wouldn't be able to see Mary's lovely smile every day. They had, therefore, agreed that he would meet her after school each night and he would walk her home.

Mary, like Jake, hadn't passed the exam and in all probability didn't even realise what it was all about, unlike Will whose parents had been priming him for weeks before.

So, it was secondary school for them, and secondary positions for life.

As the school came into sight, Will could see Mary in her usual spot at the main entrance; even from that distance he felt an inexplicable excitement. Will decided to remove his school cap which, strictly speaking, should have remained in position on his head. The rules (and as far as dress code was concerned there were many at the King Edward) stated that: 'boys would, at all times, wear the appropriate headwear when in uniform outside of the school gates until the beginning of their third school year'. This meant that once Will had arrived home tonight, he could remove it forever!

He thought,' What the hell!' and shoved it in his pocket. His stride took on a more rebellious streak. As he got closer to where Mary was patiently waiting, Will could see that she had company. He knew that one of the other three would be the ubiquitous Jake and the remainder would undoubtedly be the usual suspects:

'Waiting for dreamer boy?' enquired Jake, the biggest of the three new arrivals at the school entrance. They looked like three lost sheep.

'Yes,' demurely Mary replied, 'you know I am, I always do.' 'Why not let us walk you home?' pleaded Jake.

'Because this is what I do, and it is the only time I get to see Will.'

'Willy boy is a poof!' observed Fergie, the second in command of the group.

Fergie had become an 'admirer' and dedicated follower of Jake, after he had been 'rescued' by him on their second day at school. The school bully had taken a distinct dislike to Fergie and was about to administer his prejudicial punishment, when Jake appeared. Jake took the opportunity to build his power base and called the bully's bluff with the infamous stare (not to mention his size advantage).

Fergie was 'freed', the bully slouched away. Jake ruled. Fergie was a convert.

The third member of the contingent was a scruffy lad known as 'Drip', not for reasons of IQ, but more for the apparently continuous flow from his nose. There always seemed to be one at the end of it! He had associated himself with Jake and Fergie simply because it made him feel big. They tolerated him and he was useful, sometimes.

'Yeh,' agreed Drip, 'he's a poof!' He would have no idea what the word meant. 'Shut up you two,' Jake commanded. And instantly they did.

Will saw the 'welcoming party' congregate ahead of him, as he got ever closer to where she waited. He wasn't concerned at all because Jake would not cause any problems in front of Mary.

'Hi ya, mate,' said Will as Mary moved towards him, 'Alright?' 'I'm fine,' she always responded. Mary never did negatives. 'Fancy a walk through the park?' Will quizzed her.

'What about your homework?' she always felt obliged to ask him, knowing how important it was to him.

'Not tonight, last day of term I've got seven weeks to do that.' 'Ok the park it is then,' she said.

Jake, Fergie and Drip listened and decided that they would follow behind and re-enact the England vs Mexico match from the Saturday before.

Jake would, of course, be Bobby Charlton.

Mary and Will strolled back to the park bench which sat on the edge of the pond, where their mums had first met, and as children they had played their endless games a lifetime ago! They sat down together and were content in each other's company.

The three boys had already taken a ball from some youngsters and Bobby 'Jake' Charlton had scored his wonder goal another dozen times, including twice in the water!

They were very loud but 'silent' to Mary and Will.

'What do you want from your life, Mary?' Will innocently enquired. A question which was so natural in his household where planning was everything. Mary had been raised to appreciate today and then tomorrow would take care of itself.

'I've not ever really thought about it,' she embarrassingly replied. 'What about you?' she cleverly turned the question.

'Well,' started Will, who knew exactly what he wanted, 'first I'll complete my 'O' levels, then go to Wilberforce College to do A-levels and then onto University,' he replied.

'Then I'll begin my journey,' he said confidently.

'Journey, what journey?' Mary asked. She had heard this a thousand times before, but it was Will's certainty of his fate that always made her ask again.

'My journey of discovery around the world. America, Asia, Far East, Middle East, Africa with so much to see, to touch, to smell and to taste. Think of those creatures waiting for our eyes and mind to drink in, those sights to behold, all those people waiting to be met. All that love to be shared and received! Say you'll come with me?'

'Me!' she gasped.

'Don't be daft Will, you'll meet someone at uni and soon forget me and disappear with her.' 'I swear that no one will ever take your place, whoever I meet' Will replied.

'Why won't you think about it?' he pleaded as he had done a thousand times before. 'Because.' Was all she ever replied.

A ball suddenly crashed against the back of the seat, shocking the two of them out of their deep conversation.

A sheepish looking Drip had been sent by Jake to retrieve the ball which had miscued by about 50 yards whilst again attempting to emulate Bobby Charlton's wonder goal!

'Careful,' said Will, 'That could've hit us.'

'It was Jake, not me,' explained Drip, who as usual was only the messenger boy.

'Time to go I think,' said Mary sensing that this would be the first of many intrusions of the evening.

'Yes, let's go,' reluctantly agreed Will. 'I'll walk you home.'

They walked through the park, back toward the estate in silence for a while. They were comfortable in each other's company and had no reason to interrupt the beautiful evening's sights and sounds with any words. The 'England v Mexico' match was well out of earshot by the time they reached Mary's house.

'Think about coming with me Mary?' Will asked as he had done many times before. 'OK,' was the reply she always returned.

Will knew different. Mary knew different. They parted with a mutual 'See ya.'

Chapter 10

'Come on Will, it's about to start!' shouted Susan who, if the truth was told, was far more interested in the World cup final than Will. He much preferred playing to watching.

'Coming,' he replied, putting away his book before ambling downstairs to join the rest of the family in their spacious lounge.

Mags and John were already seated in front of the new, colour TV bought especially for the match. Susan sat cross legged immediately in front of the screen and even James had decided that it was too important an event to miss.

The Browns loved nothing more than being together on such an historic occasion.

Will arrived somewhat reluctantly but quickly entered into the spirit of the proceedings and was soon screaming at the men in red.

'Why are we playing in bleedin' red?' enquired Joe, 'We're the bleedin' home team, should be the bleedin' Krauts in red not us!' he argued with himself.

'How do you know they're playing in red?' queried Jenny, looking at the black and white screen of their TV.

'Cos I read it in the bleedin' paper this morning and you can see they're not in bleedin' white, woman!' retorted Joe.

Neither Jake nor his mum were really listening to Joe's reply, as the Germans had just opened the scoring, and they were kicking every ball as England searched for an equaliser.

'Who won the bleedin' war, anyway? Joe still continued with his rant against the Germans and the colour of England's shirts.

'Yeeeessssssssss!' screamed the entire Brown family as Hurst sublimely headed in the quickly taken free kick from the exquisite boot of the England captain Bobby Moore. Will danced round the sitting room like a demented rabbit, Mags and John enveloped each other while Susan gave her older brother a very rare kiss!

'Told ya we'd beat this bleedin' lot!' Joe stated with a smack of smugness on his face as he slurped some Watney's bitter from a 'Party Seven'.

'No, you didn't,' bravely replied Jenny, 'You said we'd get thrashed!' 'What the hell do you know, woman?' Joe bellowed.

'This is a man's game, get me another beer.' He continued.

Jake was just enthralled in the game; he loved his football and kicked every ball.

Jenny did as she was told, although in reality she was the real football fan in the house, and it was her love and interest of the game which she had passed on to Jake.

Joe just liked shouting, drinking and believing that if it hadn't been for his knee problem, he could have been playing at Wembley today!

'Half-time Mags, get the kettle on!' politely suggested John to Mags who was now curled up on the settee, totally engrossed in the unfolding drama.

'I'll make the tea,' dutifully interrupted Susan. 'Who wants one?' she continued as four hands shot up, with nobody taking their eyes from the screen.

Joe burped loudly as the second half kicked off. Jenny glared at him in disgust as Jake edged nearer to the front of his seat on the well-worn settee which he shared with his mum. Joe, as always, sat in his armchair directly in front of the TV. It was only a black and white one and had been 'acquired' from the back of a lorry.

Jake didn't really understand what that meant but, for now, he didn't care.

Even Joe smiled as he leapt from his armchair spilling the dregs of his beer over the mat. He grabbed Jake and Jenny and squeezed them as he celebrated a Martin Peter's half volley which put England ahead for the first time. Jenny and Jake embraced each other as Joe went to get his own beer for a change. He actually danced to the kitchen grinning like a Cheshire cat, grabbed another beer and came out with yet another one of his philosophical statements:

'Now let's see what you're made of you bleedin' Krauts!' 'What's a Kraut?' innocently enquired Jake.

'Just another one of your father's lovely expressions.'

whispered Jenny.

'I bleedin' heard that!' said Joe.

'That'll do nicely' agreed Will after the mammoth celebrations had settled down at the Browns' and the historic match continued to unfold in front of them.

'How long to go now?' a nervous Susan asked her Dad. 'Can't be too long now' he said looking at his watch.

'About a minute,' he continued, as the Germans were awarded a free kick.

'Just keep 'em out for this free kick, and we're the bleedin' World Champs my son!' declared Joe as he ruffled Jake's hair

The Browns and Kirkes watched simultaneously and in, apparent, slow motion as somehow the ball from the free kick squirmed into the net.

They had equalised, England were not World Champions as Joe had promised but now had another thirty minutes to endure. Then again how many promises had Joe made and broken to Jake?

The Browns sat in stunned silence.

'Get me another bleedin' beer!' slurred Joe, breaking the same silence in the Kirke household.

'Get it yourself,' bodly responded Jenny, her bitter disappointment somehow converted into bravery. 'I'm not moving' she continued. Jake was crying, he so wanted to be a World Champion when he re-enacted the game tonight with Fergie and Drip.

'It's only a game,' stupidly observed James who was a fan just for the day. Four cushions rained down on him.

'We've won it once, now let's do it again!' emphatically declared Mags, forever the optimist. Extra time commenced and both families shared a common silent prayer.

'Of course it crossed the bleedin' line, even Ray, bleedin', Charles could see that!' Joe screamed at the Russian linesman as the referee ran across to consult him after Hurst's shot had dropped down 'over the goal line'.

'Yes, but will he give it?' Jenny and Mags asked of their respective husbands simultaneously.

The yells, screams and uncontrolled leaping about in both households answered the question.

The Browns went mental. The Kirkes went mental. The nation went mental.

'Told ya!' said Joe without an expletive in sight. 'We are the World, bleedin', Champions!' he slurred.

'Not yet, Dad,' cautioned Jake, who had been disappointed once already today. Every face was riveted on the screen in front of them as the final minute arrived.

'Some people are on the pitch they think it's all over' and as Geoff Hurst smashed home the final nail in the German's coffin, the commentator's voice completed his sentence:

'...it is now!'

One minute later the whistle blew. England were indeed The World Champions of Football.

A silent second passed as the impact seeped into everyone's head. Will was the first to react at the Browns' gathering as he jumped up punching the air, grinning from ear to ear and cuddling anyone he could grab. The Browns shared a moment of sheer pleasure as they displayed their noisy excitement.

Jake had beaten Will only by a millisecond to his leap and punch in the air. He grabbed his Mum who suddenly looked beautiful as she smiled for the first time in a long, long time. They dissolved in the shared, sheer pleasure of that historic moment.

Joe snored.

He had succumbed to the alcohol seconds before the result was sealed. Neither Jenny nor Jake noticed him; this was their moment.

Outside, car horns sounded, and people were dancing in the street. Life in England was good.

Chapter 11

'What's all that noise outside, Mary?' asked Carol of her eldest daughter.

'No idea,' replied Mary as she peered through the curtains. 'But there's a lot people out there dancing about and others in cars sounding their horns. I think Will mentioned something about a match today, but I wasn't really listening.'

'Switch the telly on and find out, will you?'

'Ok' said Mary, as she pushed the button on their TV. It took several minutes to warm up before crackling into action:

'England are the World Champions after their stunning 4-2 victory against West Germany at Wembley,' announced the news reader in his classic BBC voice.'

'Yes, we won a football match, Mum, apparently we are World Champions.'

'Oh, is that all!' replied Carol, not in the slightest bit interested. No one in their household had any interest in football; it might have been different if Roy had been around. In fact, Carol knew he would have been enthralled by the match and would have been so proud to be English that day. Roy would have lived every kick and been outside celebrating with the rest. Carol paid respect to her thoughts, wiped away a tear and, as usual, got on with her life.

'Don't forget you are working in the shop for the next two weeks,' she reminded Mary. 'No Mum, not with you reminding me every five minutes!' she replied.

'Sorry love, but you know how good Mr. Smith has been to us after your dad died, and I need a break. I can spend some time with Lizzie, and you can earn a bit of cash.'

'And get touched up by Mr. Smith!' she added to her Mum's list.

'I know what he's like, but it's only men for you, they don't always think with their brains! Carol declared. 'Try to laugh it off, for me.'

'I do Mum, but he should know better at his age, how old is he anyway?' Mary enquired. 'Not really sure, but he must be well passed retirement age. Trouble is, he has nobody to carry on the business. He had no children. He has his sweet shop and us.

Lizzie burst into the room and disturbed the peace. 'What'll we do when Mary is working, Mum. Can we go swimming?'

'We can do whatever you want Lizzie, it's our fortnight together.

Chapter 12

John Brown's factory would be closed for the next two weeks as was customary for all factories. He was pleased because it had been a productive year, but he was feeling the strain. His own father had now relinquished all control of the day to day running of the factory and only 'poked his nose' in occasionally. James was already learning the business, working whenever he could in school holidays, but would soon be off to Oxford for the next three years. He had, naturally, come through A-levels with straight 'A's and then passed the entrance exam to Balliol College. He would read Economics, Politics and History'. His father hoped that after graduation he would enter the business and give some much-needed relief to John's stress levels.

James had other plans. John suspected that James had other plans.

John definitely needed a break from the factory and was so thankful of his own Father's forethought of buying the villa on the Spanish Island of Majorca. It provided an annual escape for him and his family. They had spent every 'factory fortnight' there since the twins were able to walk. It was paradise on earth, and they loved being together as a family: swimming, resting, exploring, laughing and most importantly loving. John and Mags never failed to remind their offspring that 'you get precisely what you work for'. They were never allowed to take anything in their lives for granted. To their individual credit it could be seen from their excitement, as soon as they landed in Spain, that they appreciated every experience on offer: the sun, the sky, the trees, the language, the food, the people and the unreadable notices in the windows of the shops and restaurants. They knew they were very privileged and that they should take in every experience on offer.

After the 'exertions' of the match everyone's minds concentrated on the holiday. Normally they would have flown that day, but nobody wanted to be anywhere but England for the final and so John and Mags had decided to fly out on Sunday. It meant a concerted effort to get packed and ready to leave at 4am on Sunday morning.

Together they would do it as usual.

'Why can't we have a holiday, Dad?' innocently enquired Jake.

'Cos we can't bleedin' afford it!' an awakening Joe replied, belching as he did so. 'That bleedin' poof Brown only pays us the bare minimum and then pisses off to Spain with his lazy bastard family!'

'That's not fair, Joe, they are a lovely family and work hard for what they have.' Jenny declared.

'Piss off woman and get me some dinner, I'm bleedin' starving here. Who won the match? Not those bleedin' Krauts?'

'We won, just like you promised, Dad,' responded

Jake 'We are World Champions and I'm gonna be Geoff Hurst tonight when we play footie,' he continued.

'Good lad,' said Joe again ruffling Jake's hair as if that somehow made up for all Joe's shortcomings and increased their father/son bond.

'I'll take you on an expedition next week,' added Joe. 'Where to, Spain?' hopefully asked Jake

'No, no need to fly where we are going.'

Jake looked excited. Jenny looked suspicious. Joe looked knowingly.

'Everyone ready?' asked a surprisingly alert Mags at 2.30am, 'The taxi's here!' she continued. Four affirmatives told her all she needed to know.

'Everywhere locked?' she asked of John, 'all windows shut?' she added knowing full well what he would answer.

'Yes dear,' he dutifully replied as the taxi sped off airport bound and toward their family paradise.

Chapter 13

It was 2.30am and Jake was in a deep sleep, when suddenly he felt a hand over his mouth and a gentle shake.

'Come on sleepy head, wake up it's time for our expedition.' whispered Joe.

A bleary-eyed Jake slowly came awake and realised he wasn't dreaming but his Dad was kneeling by his bed and was whispering to him.

He had only ever heard his Dad shout. 'What is it? Where are we going?' he asked.

'A little trip for me and you.' said his Dad, still in an unusually quiet voice. 'Is Mum coming too?' he innocently enquired.

'No, she bleedin' isn't.' Joe replied getting irritated and back to his normal self.

'Now get dressed and hurry up, and don't wake your Mum or I'll bleedin' belt you!' Joe whispered angrily.

Jake got the message and did as he was told.

'Right let's go, son.' Joe instructed as they left the

house by the back door.

Joe had a small bag and a torch. He wore a balaclava and gloves although it was a warm night. Jake followed behind quite excited by the thought of going out with his Dad in the middle of the night. They walked through the all too familiar estate passing the shops and the pub. Hardly anyone was about at that time and only the street lights broke the darkness. They passed a drunk who was covering the pavement with his stomach contents at the time and he didn't even notice them.

'Where are we going, Dad?' asked Jake.

'Not far, head through the park.' replied Joe.

As they entered the park, Joe turned on his torch and illuminated the footpath. This took them past the pond and towards the entrance which led to 'The Rise'.

'Why are we going to 'The Rise', Dad?'

'That's where the fun begins.' Joe responded.

They left the darkness of the park and entered 'The Rise' which, like their own estate, was well lit, although unlike on their own estate they didn't pass any drunks. The houses were also much bigger and most had a car parked on the drive.

'This is it,' observed Joe as they approached a large four bed roomed house with a wide, circular, gravelled drive. Two cars were parked in front of the house.

'This is Will's house, why are we here?' worryingly, wondered Jake to himself before plucking up the courage to ask his Dad the same question.

'Brownie asked me to keep an eye on it while he was

in Spain, and I thought the best time to have a look was at night.' Joe replied with some odd logic. Jake seemed satisfied, although he knew that Will's Dad and his own Dad were not the best of 'mates'.

They went to the back of the property, out of range of the street lights. 'Did he leave you the key, Dad?'

'Course he bleedin' did, he wanted me to look after the house, how else we would get in?' lied Joe.

A few weeks earlier Joe had taken advantage of an accident at work to sneak into John Brown's office, rifle through his jacket, which as usual hung on the back of his chair and steal his house keys.

The accident was serious. Sid Barrett, a long serving employee of Brown's, had caught his hand in one of the cutting machines and lost a finger. John had had to drive him immediately to the local hospital. He didn't need to take his jacket.

For Joe this was a bonus as it gave him time to 'borrow' a bike and speed down to the ironmongers on the estate. He had the backdoor key copied. He was back at work and the keys were safely returned to the jacket on the chair well before John returned.

'How's Sid?' Joe caringly asked of the returning boss.

'Pretty shocked,' replied John somewhat surprised that Joe should care.

'He lost one finger and was pretty lucky really, could've been the whole hand, he told me he hadn't put the guard in place.'

The guard still remained attached to its storage point on the side of the cutting machine.

'Right hand or left?' asked Joe.

'Left,' immediately returned John, again surprised at Joe's apparent interest.

'Well that's ok, he'll still be able to pick his bleedin' nose,' said Joe laughing loudly at his own joke.

John ignored the remark returning to his office and checking his keys were in his jacket pocket.

Joe opened the back door and entered with the torch flashing around. Jake innocently turned on the kitchen light.

'What the hell are you doing you dipshit?' Joe shrieked switching off the light.

'I thought you said you're looking after the house, why can't we put the light on?' asked Jake. 'We don't want the bleedin' neighbours thinking burglars are about and then ringing the police, do we?'

'Suppose not,' conceded Jake.

'Right I'm going upstairs you stay here and keep hold of this torch.'

Joe went up the stairs towards the master bedroom. He had his bag with him. Jake sneakily followed him up and as Joe entered the main bedroom Jake saw a notice on another door which read:

'WILL'S ROOM, ENTER AT YOUR PERIL'

He went in and shone the torch about. There were pictures on the walls around the neat bedroom, depicting all sorts of animals and insects. In pride of place, above the bed, was a picture of the England football team. There were rows of books on shelves and a desk, just like the

48

ones at school, up against the wall. A cup full of pens and pencils stood on top of a tatty looking book. The cover of the booked stirred something in Jake and he picked it up.

A dried and squashed butterfly silently and secretly slipped out onto the floor.

Jake looked at the picture of 'Janet and John' on the front cover of the book, and he noticed some spidery, childish writing which declared: 'Will Brown loves Mary', although even Jake noticed that the 'loves Mary' had been written by a different hand and in a different colour. Jake remembered where he had last seen this book but wondered why Will still had his.

'Jake, where the hell are you now?' anxiously asked Joe.

'Just coming Dad, what are you doing?' Jake replied, quickly returning the book to its position. 'Checking around.' replied Joe, hastily zipping up the bag before putting Mags' empty jewellery box back into her top drawer. 'What's that horrible smell in here?'

'I had a bleedin' shit, ok?' snappily answered Joe. 'Now let's get out of here.' 'Don't we need to check every room?'

'No, we've done enough tonight. Let's go,' said Joe. 'Carry this bag for me.' he instructed Jake.

The latest instruction being Joe's insurance against being stopped. Jake's role in the expedition being simultaneously defined by this action.

They left the house and Joe locked the door. Jake was still concerned about that smell. They walked back through 'The Rise' and entered the park. As they hurriedly passed the pond Jake thought he heard a 'plop' but assumed it was just a duck

Joe had thrown the key back over his head into the pond.

They arrived home.

'Give me the bag,' demanded Joe 'and you've been in bed all night, ok?' he continued, eyeing Jake with that evil glare that Jake had witnessed so many times before, usually directed at his mum.

Jake crept into his still warm bed and fell asleep. Joe farted loudly and snored immediately as his head hit the pillow next to his wife.

Jenny hadn't slept since they left the house.

Chapter 14

'Why do they have to do that?' sniffled Mags, stifling back her welling tears.

'It's very common I'm afraid to say Madam,' replied Sergeant Whelan, as he lifted a pair of Mags' 'Marks and Spencer's' finest with his pen to reveal the origin of the smell which had first alerted Susan to the break-in.

The Browns had just arrived home after a wonderful holiday in sun-drenched Spain. Their skin colour well summed up by the family name! Susan was so excited to be home and had asked for the key before the taxi had ground to a halt outside the house. She opened the door and the odour hit her straight away. John tracked the offending 'deposit' to his wife's underwear drawer.

He immediately phoned 999.

'It's a reaction to the adrenaline rush during the burglary, they have a need to empty their bowels and as often as not they do not use the obvious facility,' continued Sergeant Whelan, as he unearthed the fetid series of turds neatly curled inside a pair of Mags' St Michael's knickers.

'Shall I discard everything in this drawer Madam?'

enquired the Sergeant.

'Yes please,' immediately responded Mags, grimacing with disgust at the thought of ever having to wear them again.

'You go down and explain what's happened to the children I'll deal with the Sergeant,' thoughtfully said John to his distraught wife.

'What's missing, Sir?' enquired the Sergeant.

'They've taken all the contents of my wife's jewellery box,' said John 'I can't see anything else.'

'She never actually wore any of it, but it was left to her by her Mother and so it was kept in the drawer, just in case' he continued.

'Any idea of the value?' the Sergeant maintained his sensitive line of questioning.

He had seen too many burglaries in his twenty years on the force. He never ceased to be disgusted by the intrusion of privacy by uninvited 'guests' especially ones with no manners.

'Not really, but her Father would know the exact value as he had had it all insured when his wife was alive, but we never bothered as Mags wouldn't wear any of it. Although I do know one of the rings was worth at least a thousand pounds.' said John.

'I expect we'll never see it again?' he continued.

'They obviously wore gloves, they somehow got in without damaging anything, might have had access to a key. Any obvious ideas?' quizzed the Sergeant.

'Well I employ 150 people at the factory so I'm bound

to have one or two enemies!' answered John, 'It could be anyone,' he continued.

'We'll let the 'Crime Scene' boys have a look and I'll call into the factory next week, but I think it's unlikely we'll ever be able to prove anything.'

'Thanks for everything Sergeant. I'm just glad that nothing else has been touched and once the drawer is cleaned, we can start to move on' said John.

'You might want to consider an alarm system of some sort, I'll arrange for our 'Crime Prevention Officer' to come to see you,' the Sergeant said as he left the house.

John shook his hand, repeated his thanks and shut the door.

The Browns would, as usual, pull together as a family.

Will entered his room and looked round. There didn't, at first glance, seem to have been any intrusion into his privacy. Not that he had anything of value in his bedroom.

Then he noticed:

His cup of pens and pencils had been moved. He knew its exact position because he always placed it over where Mary had added 'loves Mary' to his name on the front of the book. She had written the addition on the cover of the book because it housed the butterfly that meant so much to both of them. Will lifted off the cup and picked up the book, it opened almost automatically to the very page.

It was missing.

All that remained inside was the imprinted stain of years of being pressed between two pages. He had deliberately forgotten to hand in the book at the end of his first year at Saint John's Infant school. It had sat on his desk as a reminder of a very special day. The day he had realised, even at that age, that there was something special about Mary. The butterfly represented that special 'something', at least to him. He looked around his room and saw it; peacefully at rest on his bedroom floor. He carefully picked it up and returned it to its rightful resting place. He put the book back on his desk and set the cup of pens and pencils on top of those words.

He knew who had been in that room.

Chapter 15

The 'Sweet Shop', as it was affectionately known, was in fact a Newsagent and Tobacconist. It had been built with the other shops in the Parade in 1951 as the new 'Mile End' council estate was being simultaneously developed. The shop neatly nestled between the Post Office and the Ironmongers. It had always been the centre of attraction for everyone.

Cedric and his wife Sheila had, for as long as they could remember, been keen on running their own business and when the opportunity arose to lease the shop from the council they didn't hesitate.

They had no ties. They had never been blessed with children.

Cedric, a name he never gave out lightly, had always been a devotee of the pipe and liked to boast that he could distinguish Erinmore 'Flake' from its sister form 'Ready Rubbed'. The idea of running a tobacconist was a dream come true. Sheila loved children and the thought of spending her days selling 'Lucky Bags' and quarters of 'Dolly Mixtures' to the young customers would be an equally satisfying dream.

They moved in as soon as the shop was finished in August 1951 and for five years their life was idyllic. They took to the shop with a natural flair based on Cedric's love of tobacco and Sheila's genuine love of children. They had had to learn all about newspapers!

Cedric, always known as Mr. Smith, quickly established a reputation as an expert in all things tobacco. People came to seek his advice on pipes and cigars, in particular. Of course, he satisfied the 'Woodbine' brigade, but he was at his happiest talking to the 'more discerning clientele' as he called them.

'You're nothing but a snob, Cedric Smith,' his doting wife observed on more than one occasion, usually accompanied with a wry smile.

He always returned her 'compliment' with an affectionate kiss on the cheek and a touch of her behind. He was a very tactile man.

The shop had a curved counter, behind which the Smiths stood, almost divided by the door behind them which led into the storeroom. A staircase at the back of the store further led up to their two-bedroomed flat above the shop.

Sheila looked after the banks of glass jars containing all manner of coloured and shaped confectionery items, all primed and ready for 'dispensing'. There were 'Dolly Mixtures', 'Love Hearts', 'Black Jacks' and 'Pear Drops' as well as mints, cough sweets and humbugs for the older customers. They sat on the shelves like well marshalled troops, patiently waiting to be weighed into the silver scoop and poured into paper bags, before being exchanged to an expectant child who handed over their sweaty coins from a tiny hand. Sheila never ceased to wonder at the delight on a young face when presented with a few sweets in a brown paper bag.

She loved it.

Cedric presided over his 'half of the counter' where the rows and rows of labelled jars containing every imaginable tobacco stood on the shelves behind him. The racks of pipes were his pride and joy. The accessories for inhaling the 'wonders of burning tobacco' were all in front of him. He knew every item intimately. The 'Rizla' papers, the pipe cleaners, the tobacco pouches and the 'roll your own machines', as Sheila called them, together with everything else the smoker could desire was there. The packets of 'Woodbine' and 'Senior Service' were always on display, together with his jar of 'single smokes', as he referred to them, were available for those who could only afford one or two 'ciggies' at a time. Thursday, the day before pay day, was the best day for promoting this particular service.

He loved it.

Then it happened. Sheila died.

It came out of nowhere on a day which started normally with the usual morning rush. The day had begun with the early morning madness: papers arriving at 5am, papers to be checked and sorted into the bags for the boys to deliver, early morning workers coming in to pick up their daily 'fags' and papers.

It was mayhem. But they loved it, together.

Then as school time approached Sheila's side of the shop went into overdrive. By 9 o'clock they were both ready for their cuppa.

After the respite it was back to work. Sheila began to stock up her jars and as she stretched up to reach the 'Fisherman's Friends' an intense pain screeched across her chest and stabbed her in the heart. She collapsed in agony and crashed to the floor behind the counter. Cedric rushed to help, and he tried everything he could remember from a long, hitherto, forgotten army first aid course attended many years before.

No first aid would have saved Sheila; she had died immediately the attack struck. Her heart could not have resisted. The doctor was so sympathetic and explained to the distraught Cedric that his efforts could not have saved her.

Cedric was devastated.

He closed the shop for a fortnight and went to Harrogate to stay with a cousin. He thought long and hard about what he should do. Eventually his decision was made when he asked himself, 'What would Sheila have done?' She, of course, would have continued their dream in his memory. Cedric decided that he would reciprocate his own thought. He would carry on in her memory and he promptly returned to the shop.

A year passed and seven assistants later Cedric was getting desperate for help. The latest of his long line of help had left. She was fed up with his constant references to his wife and how she would do things. Cedric had also developed 'wandering hand syndrome', which didn't help him keep his female workers. Cedric didn't believe that working at that end of the counter was a suitable job for a man. Besides which, he craved the company of a woman.

He had, of course, heard that Mrs Rodgers had recently and tragically lost her husband Roy. In fact, Roy had been a good customer, calling in most mornings for his paper and every Friday night to get a bag of mixed sweets, 'for my Princess Mary', as he always informed Sheila.

Whenever she visited the shop he took the trouble to serve her, usurping his authority over his current assistant. He was taken by how Carol, he had discovered her first name by now, struggled with a baby and the four-year-old Mary into the shop. She only came in once a week; on a Friday and would buy a bag of mixed sweets for Mary. Carol always seemed to struggle to find the money and his heart went out to her. He would either give her a double weight or, as often as not, he would simply pretend to give her change but actually gave her the same amount of coins back as she had handed over. She always smiled back at him as she returned the money to her purse. He would come around the counter and tickle Lizzie's chubby baby cheeks and smile at Mary, who by now was tucking into her 'Flying Saucers'. Cedric always opened the shop door for Carol and her girls and bid them 'Goodnight' with a slight touch of his forehead.

Following the departure of his latest helper who cited his over exuberant use of hands as the reason to leave, Cedric was at his wits end as to how he would cope.

It was a Friday and in walked Carol.

She said 'Yes' as soon as he asked her, without really thinking about what she would do with the girls. Mr. Smith had agreed to allow her to work as freely as she needed around the girls. Carol knew her Mother would help, and the thought of that extra money was the clincher.

So began their 'relationship' behind the counter. Carol tolerated his touching and the occasional rubbing in exchange for the freedom to work around her beloved daughters.

Chapter 16

Cedric could usually find holiday relief when Carol needed a break, but in that summer of 1966, he could find nobody. It was Carol who first suggested Mary.

'She's thirteen now and I'm sure she'll soon pick it up.'

They agreed that Mary would have a trial run on a couple of Saturday mornings alongside Carol and if things worked out then Mary could come in for 'factory fortnight'.

The trial period went very well. Mr. Smith was impressed with Mary's attitude. Her budding attributes were an additional bonus.

'Morning Mr. Smith,' smiled Mary on arrival that first Monday morning of Carol's holiday. 'And a very good morning to you too, Mary,' replied Cedric.

They shared the counter exactly as he had with his wife and of course with Carol. Mary soon noticed how often he squeezed past her when there was a bit of a lull in the shop; fortunately, these lulls were few and far between. Carol had explained about Mr. Smith and 'his ways' and about men in general. Mary was developing as a woman and was well aware of the 'birds and bees' as her mum called it! She tolerated Mr. Smith because, since her mum had worked in the shop, life had been good.

The two weeks went by quickly and of course it took her mind off Will.

She had noticed the boys playing football outside the shop on what everyone referred to as 'The Green'. 'The Green' was an area of grass opposite the parade of shops. It was like an island surrounded by a road. It wasn't originally designed for football, but its circular shape made the boys think it was Wembley, and there weren't too many cars around to worry about.

Jake, Fergie and Drip always seemed to appear at the door every evening just as Mary left the shop.

'Can I walk you home, Mary?' Jake asked on that first Monday.

'I'd like that,' replied Mary. Jake smiled. He stared at Fergie and Drip with a jerked movement of his head which meant 'go away'.

They did as he indicated. They always did.

Jake and Mary would walk back to the estate through the park without a great deal of conversation. Jake was just pleased to be with her, he wasn't a big talker. In fact, Mary always had to lead any conversation. Unlike when she walked with Will, who could chat for England! Jake made Mary feel confident. She, in turn, was undemanding and gave him mental protection. They would sit on the seat overlooking the pond, where she had spent hours with Will. It was different, but in its way just as comfortable.

'What plans do you have for the future?' she would

ask Jake, just as Will had asked her many times.

'Dunno,' Jake would respond. A short, sharp response was Jake's standard reply to anything, especially when he felt inferior.

'What'll you do when you leave school?' she continued, hoping for a more elaborate response.

'Dunno,' he would answer.' S'pose I'll work in the factory with Dad.'

Jake didn't know how to plan, he was happy to get through today and worry about tomorrow when it happened. This is how Mary felt whenever she was near Will.

They returned to the more comfortable state of silence as Mary looked out over the water.

Mary noticed the dragonfly. Jake didn't. She saw the fish in the pond reach for air. Jake didn't. She watched as a butterfly flickered by. Jake knew he'd seen one somewhere recently, but he didn't remember it flying.

They would sit for half an hour and then continue their stroll back to Mary's house. An awkward Jake would say 'Bye, see you tomorrow night?' hopefully.

'See you after work,' Mary would answer.

Jake would run off, with a glimmer of pleasure across his face, to join Fergie and Drip who never seemed to be far away.

This ritual continued for the two weeks that Mary worked in the shop for Mr. Smith. Then on her last day, as they approached the pond as usual, there he was:

Mary spotted him first and her heart raced. The first

thing she noticed was how blond his hair had become and how it was slightly longer. Then, as she got closer, she saw his skin colour. He was a wonderful chocolate brown colour. He looked Spanish. She had never seen him look so 'beautiful'. She meant that word.

Jake saw him too: The first thing he noticed was his 'poofy' hair colour, it was like a woman's. He's dyed it he thought. Then as he got closer, he saw his skin colour. It was an ugly black. He looked like a greasy wop. He meant those words.

The seeds were being sown. Jealousy and bigotry are comfortable bed fellows.

'I've got to find the boys,' he excused himself and ran off to find Fergie and Drip. Mary was puzzled but continued towards the pond.

Mary and Will embraced clumsily and laughed. They sat by the pond for two hours talking and watching. They each covered every minute of their respective time apart.

Will painted a fantastic picture of his family holiday in Spain. Mary heard about the sun, the sea, the beach, the laughter and his family simply being together. Mary could only listen in wonder; she had no comparative experiences to draw on. She could not get over the colour of his skin; she had never seen anyone, naturally white, so bronzed by the sun. Her fortnight seemed insignificant by comparison, but Will wanted to hear it all. He thought it was brilliant that she had worked in the shop and got to meet so many people. He was disturbed when she mentioned some of Mr. Smith's 'touching' habits. Mary dismissed these as nothing and said it was just the actions of a lonely old man who didn't mean any harm.

As the evening drew in, it got a bit cooler and Will remarked, 'Let's move before they raise the parking rate!' Mary laughed at Will's silly joke.

They strolled back through the park towards Mary's house on the estate and carried on talking. Will didn't see any point in mentioning the break-in and certainly not in telling her who he suspected was involved. Anyway, Will didn't believe that Jake had carried it out by himself. It would all come out eventually.

He saw her to her front door and said 'See ya,' as usual but unusually, and for the first time, he kissed her on each cheek. Just as had seen the Spanish house keeper do to his Mum and Dad when they were greeted on arrival at the holiday villa.

Will felt it was so natural a thing to do. Mary felt so good. She smiled and waved to him as she entered her front door.

Chapter 17 ~ 1969

The world watched and waited in total awe at the drama unfolding before them. They switched on their grainy black and white TVs, knowing they were joined by millions of people around the world doing exactly the same thing, at precisely the same time.

The Browns were a part of those millions. They sat together and watched and waited with the rest of the world. They also looked on in colour. There was no chance that any of them would miss this unique occasion, and witnessing it together made it even more special. Just like three years earlier when England had won the World Cup so dramatically.

James, Susan and Will sat together on the large sofa in the spacious lounge, each one of them in total silence as the real-life drama captivated their attention. John, as usual, sat in his armchair with Mags on the floor in front of him. His hand rested on her shoulder and she leaned against his thighs, still as firm as when she first met him in the library, all those years ago. Her eyes met his and then travelled around the room looking at their three beautiful offspring. She loved this family, she loved this house and she loved being together. The children took for granted that John and Mags were so affectionate in their presence, they didn't even notice when John leaned forward and kissed the back of their Mum's head. She did and reached back to pat his cheek. John smiled inwardly and felt proud of his family as they waited for the moment:

'That's one small step for man, one giant leap for mankind,' announced Neil Armstrong as he left the lunar module, 'The Eagle', and put the first human foot on the surface of the moon.

The world watched with the Browns. The Browns watched together. They sat in complete amazement, each trying to take in the enormity of the event. Will broke the silence, as they watched Neil bouncing along his dusty path:

'Doesn't look real to me,' he nonchalantly announced. He was greeted with unanimous derision, and his observation was ignored.

'Is everyone here for dinner?' announced Mum, who thought two hours of any moon landing is enough for anyone!

'Yes,' replied everyone in unison.

'I'm out with Sam tomorrow though,' said Will, as an afterthought and as if it had any relevance to his Mother's present culinary question.

Nobody was listening to him anyway, not after his previous remark!

Chapter 18

The needle crackled as it moved across the first few millimetres of the black plastic, which simultaneously spun around on the turntable of the tiny 'Dansette' record player.

'Get up in the morning, slaving for bread sir, so that every mouth can be fed,' announced 'Desmond Decker' from the speakers of the record player in the corner of the room.

'Poor me, the Israelite. Aah' the singer continued.

Jake knew every word of this song; he had played it to death since he'd bought it earlier that summer.

He screamed into his hairbrush, 'the Israelite!' as he 'reggaed' around the room in his white Y fronts, bobbing up and down to the sensuous, Caribbean beat majestically accompanied by that wonderful soulful accent of the black singer.

He loved this sound; the anthem of his chosen set.

It was a true irony that 'they' should associate themselves with black music.

Jake had, of course, left school at the earliest

opportunity and June 1969 had been that official opportunity. He had given up long before that, although in truth the system had given up on him.

Now Jake had a job and he had some money.

John Brown had been very reluctant to take on another Kirke at the factory. He felt he had done the world a big favour in taking one of 'them' off the streets; to have two would be far too much. Will had pleaded with his Dad to give him a chance, observing with some truth:

'It's not Jake's fault that his Dad is an arsehole!'

'William!' said Mags, 'That's enough of that sort of language!' 'Sorry, Mum but he is,' half apologised Will.

'OK,' said John, 'I give up, he can have a trial period.' 'Thanks Dad, I know that'll keep Mary happy.'

'What's Mary got to do with it?' asked John looking completely puzzled. Will had departed to tell Mary. Mags looked on knowingly.

John wasn't too bothered really because Joe Kirke had recently developed a 'back problem' and was off work as and when it suited. Joe knew how to play the wonderful welfare system, in his favour, to the limit. Joe didn't let the problem get in the way of his nocturnal 'work'. If John was honest, he would happily pay him to stay home, work life was much easier without people like Joe around.

Jake, therefore, had a job and in truth he was a much better worker than his Dad. Jake could do 'this' work, which was something he never could at school. He felt good about himself at last and as a bonus he had an income.

He could buy himself a record if he wanted and he could afford to spend money on the 'uniform'. He found it all lying neatly on his bed where his ever-attentive Mum had placed it, with one exception:

'Where's my bleedin' Ben Sherman?' he screamed downstairs, momentarily overshadowing Desmond Decker as he did so.

'In the airing cupboard,' servant-like Jenny replied.

He opened the cupboard and there, on a hangar as promised, was his pride and joy. His white 'Ben', pristine and pressed. He loved it and when he wore it, he felt superior.

'Thanks, Mum,' he shouted, wishing he hadn't sworn at her, a habit he noticed he had started since working at the factory. Dad had said it made him sound grown up.

He went back to his room and returned Desmond to full volume just as the record finished. He let the arm of the record player return to its resting place before carefully lifting off the shiny black disc from the turntable; he wiped the surface of it across the back of his Y fronts and placed it in its brown card sleeve. He picked up his second favourite record of the moment, removed it from its sleeve, repeated the wiping action and placed it carefully on the turntable of the record player. He lifted the arm and placed the needle to the edge of the disc and waited. He didn't need a hairbrush for this one, or for his hair.

The wonderful sound of that 'Ska' instrumental was enough to send Jake into another world as he bopped once more around the room in nothing but his pants. He disappeared to somewhere else as 'The Upsetters' finally 'Returned to Django'. He was free from his deficiencies, actual and perceived. He came alive. He was himself, he was equal, he was happy. He had a purpose.

'Turn that bleedin' racket down,' shouted Joe, very audible through the ceiling. Jake adjusted the volume knowing full well who would suffer if he didn't.

Jake didn't care as his eyes viewed his neatly spread clothes laid with military precision across his bed.

He put on his white 'Ben' and watched himself do up the buttons in the dressing table mirror. It felt good. He felt good as he did the final button. He loved the button-down collar and the pleat down the back. He turned back to his bed and picked up the Levi 'Sta-Prest', he slid first one leg in closely followed by the other. He did up the button and zipped the fly. His white 'Ben' was carefully tucked into the black 'Sta-Prest'. The red braces were clipped into place without thought as he looped his two thumbs into the front side of each brace. He bent at the knees and felt even better. His socks were next, red of course and were pulled into position.

He glanced down to the foot of the bed and there they were: freshly cleaned and shiny, the smell of polish hit his nostrils as he smiled. He picked them up and kissed each reinforced toe cap. 'Someone else would taste them later', he thought to himself. His 'Doc Martins', his pride and joy, his weapon of destruction. He slid his respective feet into the boots and secured the laces. He looked down and checked the gap between the bottom of his trousers and the top of his boots. It was perfect and as it should be. The uniform was completed as he slipped into his black 'Harington' which covered the braces but enhanced the whiteness of his underlying shirt. Jake's hair had been shorn that day. He dabbed a little 'Brut' on his face and winced as the alcohol hit a recently picked spot. Jake didn't need a razor but the after shave was a necessity. He was complete.

He was a true Skinhead.

He looked again into his mirror as he danced once more to Desmond 'getting up in the morning slaving for bread, sir!' He smiled inwardly to himself and left the house to meet the others.

Chapter 19

Will picked the first T-shirt he could find in his drawer and pulled it down over the top of his well-worn flared jeans. He put on his 'off white' plimsolls, shouted good bye and left the house with a slam of the front door.

Fashion, or keeping up with it, was not Will's thing!

It was a Monday night and, as usual, Will went out to meet his best friend Sam. They didn't do much; in fact, there wasn't much for two sixteen-year olds to do around 'The Rise' and 'Mile End', where they respectively lived. In fact, there was nothing for any sixteen-year olds to do.

Sam was the son of Joshua and Martha Jones. They had arrived in the country about 18 years ago from Jamaica, along with many other couples 'seeking their fortune'. Joshua, or JJ as he was affectionately nicknamed, was an extremely amiable man and had immediately found work at 'Browns'. He worked hard to support his family, which soon had the addition of a new son; they had called him Samuel after his Granddad. They had been encouraged by John Brown to put their names down on the 'Council House List'. Joshua and Martha didn't need to know that John Brown was well connected at the Council.

They were one of the first couples to move onto the new council estate and had even featured in a 'Pathe News' item showing off the new, social-living experiment in our 'Britain for All'. Joshua got on well with everyone at 'Browns', and in general he had none of the problems he had been warned about before leaving the Caribbean. Life was pretty good for the Jones.

Except for Joe Kirke.

Will and Sam were complete opposites, but they somehow found a lot of common ground which was in no short measure helped by their love of football. Will had a purpose, a 'dream' as he always described it to Mary, but that apart he was carefree and did the bare minimum to get through at school. His bare minimum was, however, way above average. Sam was intense and dedicated. He had to work hard to stand still, but like his father he wanted to make the most of his golden opportunity.

Sam and Will had met at football practice during their first term together at the King Edward grammar. They hit it off immediately both on and off the pitch. Sam was brilliant and could score for fun as he did six times during that opening match. Will was only good, and he had to work hard to keep up with Sam. Mr. Fox, the sports master, saw a partnership in the making and Will and Sam became the First Eleven's strike force. They terrorised all the local schools and even gave a university team a run for their money before losing by the odd goal in three. Sam was the star on the pitch and Will was the brains off it. They helped each other and somehow together seemed more than two people.

In the local football world, they were affectionately

known as the 'Black and White Minstrels'. Will loved Sam as a mate. His actual love was Mary. Sam loved Will.

Will didn't notice Sam observing him when they showered and sometimes Sam's hand would brush along Will's arm when they sat together putting their boots on. All Will was interested in was playing football and getting to university and on to his dream. Sam was confused, he knew he was different but became special on that pitch and life off it was good with the undemanding presence of Will.

One match stood out to both of them. The game was against a local grammar school as usual, but unusually the match had to be played at the secondary school pitch for some reason or another.

Jake, Fergie and Drip had turned up to see what was going on at their old school. They hadn't seen Will, but they did notice Sam who scored a hat trick in the first half. He was brilliant, better than anyone on the pitch. Something stirred in Jake as Sam stroked home his fourth goal of the game from a Will through ball. Jake was good too, just like Will, but this guy was special, and Jake didn't like it.

'Sambo,' he yelled, 'Do you want a banana?' Fergie and Drip laughed. Drip didn't really know what he was laughing at. As Sam's fifth of the day crashed against the back of the net, Jake began to jump up and down scratching himself under each arm and making a strange, animalistic noise:

'Oo-oo-oo!' he squealed. Fergie and Drip joined in. They looked like three demented monkeys.

The match was stopped by a loud whistle from the

referee, Mr. Fox, who calmly but sternly told the three spectators to 'stop that immediately!'. The three protagonists each muttered, 'Fuck off,' under their breaths. Jake lifted his hand clenching his thumb and his end digits; He raised the remaining two to Mr. Fox, before the three of them ran off. Sam had heard but didn't understand. Will had heard and did.

It had started.

Chapter 20

Jake swaggered down the road. He felt indestructible. He had arranged to meet Fergie and Drip by the pond in the park. They too were in uniform, except they wouldn't dare to own a 'Ben', never mind wear one in Jake's presence. That was his badge of office. They had to be content with the lower ranking 'Fred Perry'. Fergie wore white and Drip's was black. Jake was content that they knew their place.

'Did you get some?' he asked on arrival at the bench overlooking the pond. 'Yep!' replied Drip, so pleased with himself for getting something for Jake. 'How many bottles?' further enquired Jake.

'Three,' was the immediate response.

Drip's sister, Janet, worked at the local 'Co-Op', one of the estate's shops along the parade opposite the 'Green', and could usually 'acquire' things, especially when Jake had asked. He had asked and Janet had delivered: three large, glass bottles of cider. Of course, the boys would not have been able to buy the drink themselves.

'Well give me one then and let's get stuck in.'

instructed Jake. The tops were unscrewed, and they began pouring the orange liquid down their throats.

Drip didn't really like it but couldn't let the boys down. Jake finished his first, of course, and immediately threw the empty bottle into the pond. Much more satisfying than getting the bottle's deposit back! Fergie was second and copied his master's throwing action. Jake burped loudly and Drip spat a mouthful out with laughter. They all giggled in unison. Jake and Fergie helped Drip to finish his remaining cider. They all laughed loudly and had a competition to produce the loudest belch. Jake was the judge and he won. The third bottle joined the others in the aquatic burial place. They all giggled as the bottle hit the water with a thunderous 'plop', filled with water and subsequently sank.

'I need a piss,' said Drip in a somewhat slurred voice.

'So do I,' agreed Fergie, 'Let's go behind the tree,' he continued.

While they were relieving themselves, Jake sat down and stared at the pond. His head was filled with a sensation of lightness and he felt he could do anything.

'Wish she'd have got another bottle,' he thought just as the others got back. Drip was a bit unsteady on his feet now and Fergie had to catch him at one point.

'Let's go to the bleedin' chip shop,' ordered Jake, suddenly sounding like his Dad. 'Yeh, fets go to the lucking ship chop!' agreed Drip.

'What should we do tonight?' asked Will, already well aware of the answer, as he met Sam on the side of the road which separated their two estates. As was usual Sam had brought his football which, he had tucked under his arm. They always kicked a ball around for an hour or so and then went for chips on Mondays, in fact they did it every time they met, which was more often outside term time.

They went to the 'Park' and played and practiced until it started getting dark. They loved every minute and fine-tuned their skills and understanding of each other. The two 'Minstrels' wanted to be the best at anything they did.

'I desperately need a drink,' declared Will.

'Thought you'd never admit it,' smiled Sam, who was just as thirsty, but such was their competitiveness he was determined to win this one! He did.

'Let's go get chips and a coke,' suggested Sam.

The chippie was the end shop on the parade and when they arrived, they saw a few locals outside. It looked as if someone had been sick. There were discarded 'chip' papers on the path being trodden on by the 'Doc Martins' of the locals.

Will nodded at Jake as he walked past him into the shop. Jake ignored Will and glared at Sam. Sam moved quickly and followed Will into the warmth of the shop. They emerged five minutes later. They each had a bag of chips with 'crispy bits' and a bottle of Coca Cola. Will stood his drink on the wall and launched into his chips. A somewhat uncomfortable Sam followed suit.

'Give us a chip, Sambo,' snarled Jake.

'Yeh, give us a chip, monkey boy' said Fergie.

'Get your own,' replied Will on his friend's behalf.

'It's alright Will, they can have one,' said Sam holding out his paper-wrapped meal to Jake. Drip was being sick over the wall again as Jake grabbed a handful of Sam's chips.

'Not so many,' protested Sam.

'What you are going do about it?' sneered Fergie as he grabbed his own handful and simultaneously knocked into Sam causing him to spill the remainder onto the path.

Will sensed trouble as Sam bent down to retrieve what he could from the paper bag which had saved the chips hitting the concrete. As he bent a 'Doc Martin' smashed into his backside and he turned to face the boot's owner. Jake glared down at him.

'Problem, Sambo?' he enquired. Will put his own bag on the wall and confronted Jake: 'Leave us alone, we're not doing you any harm.'

'Your bleedin' monkey mate is making a mess on our estate and he needs teaching a lesson,' reasoned Jake.

Sam was still rubbing his painful backside when Drip returned from his stomach emptying exercise to show he was just as tough as Jake and gave Sam another kick.

Will immediately came to his friend's aid and pushed Drip away. As Will kneeled to help Sam to his feet, Jake and Fergie attacked in unison. Fuelled by the cider they rained fists and boots into Will and Sam who were helpless on the ground; they could do nothing but attempt to curl up and protect their heads and faces. Jake grinned, Fergie copied, and Drip revisited his chips.

Alerted by the noise Mr. Graham, the chip shop

proprietor, came running out of his shop and screamed at Jake and Fergie who were now in a violent frenzy and apparently unstoppable.

'Oi, stop!' he shouted, brandishing a baseball bat in the general direction of Jake's shaven head. Fergie stopped immediately and ran off as fast as he could. Drip stopped throwing up and joined his mate on the run of his life. Jake stopped his attack but stood his ground in front of Mr. Graham.

'Piss off or I'll call the police,' were Mr. Graham's options to Jake. Will and Sam groaned but slowly got to their feet. Jake stared into the eyes of the chip shop owner and almost dared him to use his bat.

The bat had been bought by George Graham, three years earlier, after he had been visited in the night by 'person or persons unknown'. The nocturnal visitors had cleaned out his till, after he had had a very lucrative Saturday night. George could still remember the stench of the cooked turd he had found, the next morning, floating in the fryer. He would use the bat next time but not tonight, not on a kid. Because however aggressive Jake appeared, he was, indeed, nothing more than a child. The only thing he shaved was his head!

'I'll bleedin' have you,' warned Jake. George never flinched. Jake's bravery was slowly ebbing away, especially, as he was completely on his own. Will and Sam were now standing side by side with Mr. Graham and Jake suddenly felt vulnerable. He decided 'piss off' was the best option and he turned and ran to join his earlier departed mates.

Will was rubbing his back as Sam wiped away blood

from a cut over his left eye. They had nothing broken and the shock of Jake's actions was more of a concern than any injury, especially to Will. Will had never encountered this level of hatred from Jake in the ten years of being in his presence. Although he had witnessed his nasty streak many times before, since they had first met in the Park all those years ago.

But, somehow, this was different.

'Come on boys, into the shop and have another bag of chips on me, I don't think you'll have any more trouble from those three...' said Mr. Graham.

'...tonight,' added Will, under his breath, looking at Sam. 'Why?' he wondered as his friend patted his eye with a handkerchief loaned by Mr. Graham.

The two friends took up Mr. Graham's offer and then set off for home. The injuries suffered in those few minutes of mindless violence were no worse than they had suffered in a tough match against the local secondary school. They walked home and went their separate ways at the main road.

'See ya,' said Will. 'Definitely,' replied Sam.

Chapter 21

Mary had settled well into her full-time employment and working alongside her Mum made it even better.

Cedric Smith had decided he wanted to cut down on his hours behind the counter as he approached retirement age. He had slowly involved Carol in learning more about his beloved tobacco and newsagent's world. Mary had been a willing student. She was a natural, enjoying the extra responsibility and, of course, the extra money which Cedric offered her when he told her of his plans. By the time Mary had started full time, eighteen months earlier, Carol knew all there was to know about the job. Cedric had also got to know more about Carol! He always seemed to need to be close to her, gently pushing past or brushing her breasts as he reached for some matches. Carol allowed only so much and had told him straight that no one would ever replace her beloved Roy. He seemed to accept her rejection and was just grateful for her presence.

He thoroughly enjoyed the company of the two 'Rodgers girls' as he called them and started cutting down on his time in the shop. Carol and Mary worked well together, with Mum in charge of all things tobacco and Mary looking after the 'sweet' end of the shop. They took turns doing the early shift with Cedric, who enjoyed his mornings with Mary. He noticed she was developing in all the right places and he would try his well-practiced manoeuvres. Mary had been well informed of the ways of the male of the species by her mum and put up with him, because in all other ways he was good to them. Until one day in the shop he went too far:

Mary was in the shop one afternoon, alone with Cedric, and was filling the sweet jars as usual whilst things were quiet. She was reaching up, stretching toward the 'Fruit Bonbons', when she felt two hands come from behind and cupped both breasts.

Mary turned and confronted him.

'What on earth are you doing?' angrily screamed Mary. Cedric was shocked back on his feet.

'I thought you were going to drop the jar,' he meekly explained, his face turning as red as the

'Cherry Drops'.

'Well I wasn't,' she replied.

'I'm sorry if l hurt you,' was his final comment of the afternoon.

They continued their work in silence. Cedric felt ashamed. Mary felt soiled. She had, of course, told her mother about the incident.

Carol had subsequently been obliged to speak to him. It was at that point he suggested that the girls should take over in the mornings and he would take over for the quieter, afternoon shift. This worked well and life was good for all of them.

He meant no harm; he was simply lonely and frustrated. It took Mary a long time to forgive him but as she saw him less and less, she came to terms with her experience.

Jake would call in every morning on his way to the factory to buy a paper and of course he had to buy some sweets just to speak to Mary.

'Usual?' Mary would ask.

'Yeh' was Jake's nervy reply. He was desperate to ask her out, but he was too shy. Mary weighed out the mint imperials into a bag and handed them to Jake. He thought they sounded like a grown-up purchase. He smiled, took the bag, paid and left.

At eight thirty every morning Mary would brush her hair and hope that the next customer through the door would be Will. Will was not a creature of habit and only called in on odd occasions, but you could set a clock on his timing when he did appear. He would never be late for school and always passed the shop at 8.30.

His arrival would elate Mary for the whole day. 'Usual?' Mary would ask if he appeared.

'Yes please,' was Will's confident reply. She was desperate for him to ask her out, particularly with the church Christmas disco coming up. It never crossed his mind. Mary handed the can of coke to Will. He smiled, took the can, paid and left.

Chapter 22

Will was now well settled into his A level courses at Wilberforce College.

The results of his O-levels had been delivered by post just three weeks after the infamous 'chip shop attack'. They were, as expected, brilliant! He had achieved his predicted eight grade 1s and two grade 2s and could now transfer to the College to study Biology, Chemistry and Maths. The family were delighted and set off almost immediately for their annual trip to their apartment in Spain. No sooner was the holiday over than it was time for school again.

Now Will was free to dress as he pleased; 'within reason' added the College handbook, and he even allowed his hair to take its own destiny. Will was in his element as he set out on that first day; he wore his favourite T-shirt, the one bearing the 'Led Zeppelin I' album cover design and felt so comfortable in those faded jeans. He had, as usual, tanned beautifully in Spain and his long blond hair completed his 'Adonis' appearance. Will just felt at ease with himself and looked forward to concentrating on his favourite subjects, as he ambled along the road towards the College. On the way he met, and walked with, Sam who had performed equally as well in his exams and was to embark on his own path of learning. Sam would take a different route toward the ultimate goal of University. He had a real talent for writing and drawing and to that end would study English, Art and History at Wilberforce. Neither of them was too bothered about taking completely different academic directions because their paths always crossed on the football pitch.

They played hard and worked even harder. They always avoided places they knew Jake would hang out in because he actually frightened Sam. Will wasn't particularly concerned about Jake but went along with his friend. Sam always wanted to be with Will, and he had noticed recently how odd Sam always became in Mary's presence.

Will felt 'changed' since he had started his A levels, not just the fact that he was treated more like an adult at the College, but inside himself.

He was a bit shocked to wake one morning, after a particularly restless night dreaming about Mary, to find his pyjamas soaking wet around his crotch area. He also felt a sense of pleasurable relief on waking. Will was worried the first time it occurred and secretly washed his night clothes. He soon ran out of clean pyjamas and eventually decided to speak to his mum, in case he had a problem. The Browns, Mags especially, could discuss anything. Will approached her somewhat nervously, but as soon as she smiled on hearing about his 'problem' he knew he had nothing to worry about.

Mags explained all, simply and effectively, and although Will had heard the school boy's version, of course, he was enthralled by the ease of delivery of hers. After stating the facts with her 'nature' lecture, she continued the explanation with how, alongside nature, the most important and complementary value was love. 'Making love' in love was the ultimate state. A bond of love with another human being, where two people could grow and develop together, was the most desirable state possible. Marriage was the best environment to convert that love into the greatest union between two people: children.

Will realised in that moment what his mum and dad were all about and knew that was what he wanted: all in good time.

Chapter 23

Jake had accidently found the magazine under his dad's bed when he was looking for his shoes and was intrigued by the half-naked woman on the cover. He skimmed through the pages of 'Parade' and gasped at the pictures of the uncovered female bodies on display. He felt a stirring in his pants and felt the need to touch himself. He didn't quite know what was happening and had no one to ask. His dad never had time for him between 'going out at night' and the pub, and although he loved his mum, he felt that this was a man's thing and he couldn't speak to her about it. His frustrations would be satisfied either from his own wrist or, more usually, from his boots. He always replaced the magazine but returned frequently, especially when he knew there were new ones.

He was alert to the periodic, plain brown envelope delivered by the postman, and addressed to Mr. Joseph Kirke.

Jake and the boys continued to terrorise the neighbourhood and their reputation had been greatly enhanced following the attack on Will and Sam. Their paths didn't really cross nowadays as Will and Sam were students at Wilberforce and spent most evenings at home studying. They also spent their weekends playing football while Jake, Fergie and Drip spent weekends in and around the pub. At seventeen they could get away with buying beer and if there was a problem Joe would solve it for them. After the beer had anaesthetised their collective inhibitions, they would seek out a 'hairy' or a 'paki' to punish, for simply being different. Jake was tough because he had a reputation to uphold. In truth he only loved his clothes and his music. He also loved Mary.

Chapter 24

Reverend Paul Stevens had arrived at St John's fifteen months earlier with his wife Joy and their son, Josh. They had quickly and effortlessly settled into the area. Josh was sixteen and had just completed his O-levels. It was therefore the perfect time to move to the new diocese, as Josh could simultaneously transfer to his new A-level college. So when the opportunity came up Paul and Joy decided quickly that it was the best thing for all of them.

Josh soon settled in at Wilberforce College and was a very able student of music. He played the drums in the school orchestra, which was considered 'very cool' and he quickly became popular with both sexes. He loved all types of music.

Joy was the family's musical influence. She had studied the subject at Cambridge and played any instrument she could lay her hands on, particularly the piano. She sang like a nightingale and it was hearing her play the organ in chapel that Paul had first encountered her. He fell in love simultaneously with her voice and her soul.

She was willing to share his life as a vicar's wife and what she brought musically to their partnership more than compensated, to Paul, for all her difficulties with the concept of God.

She played organ in church and the choir was all the better for her presence. Paul loved her and what she brought to his church.

Joy enveloped all music and had been sold on the so-called popular variety since the day Bill Hayley had 'Rocked around the Clock'. She devoured every '45' released and bought most of them. Her 'love' influenced the young Josh and he was exposed to every type of sound imaginable and loved it all. It was hardly surprising that he had similar tastes and a desire to study music. As with every teenager he had taken influences from his parents and fine-tuned them to his own requirements. He loved all the sounds of the day. He spent his paper round money on the single of the week, and he listened avidly to the 'Top Thirty' every Sunday waiting for the number one to be announced just before seven o'clock.

Josh had bought a pair of old turntables from a jumble sale last year and with his dad's help had connected them to some old speakers which Paul already had in the garage. They hugged each other when they finally actually got a record to play! Paul bought some disco lights from a second-hand shop and when he and Josh had added them to the turntable and speakers, they had a real disco to play with. Josh practised with his new equipment in the church hall. He had plenty of singles to play, what with his own and his mum's vast collection. He loved it.

Paul was determined, in his own way, to try to integrate the two neighbouring estates which fell under his jurisdiction. He tried, in particular, to do this by encouraging the youngsters to mix. His first initiative was the Youth Club which he ran every Tuesday in the Church Hall.

It had a mixed reaction at first. The church hall was kitted out with the usual table tennis and refreshments, but something else was needed to bridge the gap between the two estates. The two groups didn't really gel until the football team was formed. The grammar school set and the secondary set boys seemed to have little in common and Paul was always worried whenever Jake and his mates turned up. There always seemed to be an atmosphere, particularly if Sam was there. The girls were never a problem and were simply happy to meet and talk. Boys seemed to want more. It was a stroke of genius to start a football team!

It was actually Jake's suggestion. During one of his moody, disruptive appearances at the youth club he started to annoy everyone by aimlessly kicking a ball about in the hall.

'Take the ball outside, please Jake,' requested Paul as calmly as he could, after the ball had struck a window for the third time.

'Nowhere to play out there,' remarked Jake, 'We need a decent pitch and a team to play in,' he continued.

Paul thought about the comment and decided that Jake had a good idea. He contacted a couple of other local youth clubs and the idea took off. There were only seven boy regulars at the club: Josh, Will, Sam, Jake, Fergie, Drip and Sol. So they suggested starting up a seven a side mini league in the first place. The idea was a great success.

On the pitch the boys had a common cause. They trained together, they played together, they won together, and they worked together. It was weird. Off the pitch Jake hated Sam, but if anyone picked on him on the pitch, Jake was the first one there to solve any 'problem'.

The 'Black and White Minstrels' terrorised all the other teams and St. John's won every game. The togetherness was a pleasure to behold and it was a personal joy to Paul. The girls got involved on the touchline and the youth club increased in popularity as everyone wanted to be in the St John's team. There were still problems off the pitch and Paul had to step in on more than one occasion when Jake had a issue with Sam.

Chapter 25

The Christmas Disco had been Joy's original idea, but now the night had arrived the boys had taken over!

The Hall looked great on that Tuesday night three days before Christmas Day. The tree was a gift from the local Garden Centre and its lights looked stunning. Paul and Joy manned the refreshments counter and of course Josh wore the headphones. The sound was good, the flashing lights gave it a professional feel and the hall was beginning to fill up.

Will and Sam had come over early to help set up the equipment with Josh. There was a good mix of people from both estates and the atmosphere was building nicely. Mary was, as ever, the belle of the ball and surrounded by a crowd. Lizzie and Will's sister, Susan, stood in close attendance as a gaggle of boys vied for Mary's attention.

She had only eyes for one.

Will and Sam were, as usual, in deep conversation over a can of coke and both nodding their heads in time to 'Deep Purple'.

As the last chords of 'Black Night' finished and a

momentary silence hit the room, the door of the Church Hall crashed open.

There they stood in full uniform: Jake, Fergie and Drip. Paul looked across and thought, 'Oh no.' He looked at them, they looked at Sam, Sam looked to Will and Will finished his coke.

Josh reacted quickly and searched his collection; he picked up the required disc, removed it from its protective case. He carefully wiped it, placed it on the turntable and lowered the needle onto its edge. The 'crackle' resounded around the silent room and seemed to last for ever as the stylus travelled across to the first groove of the record:

'Get up in the morning, slaving for bread, sir!' screamed around the room breaking the silence. Everyone was momentarily startled except Jake.

He was transformed.

His stare turned into a serious grin as he strutted across the room and stood by himself in the centre of it. He began dancing to, and mouthing with, every word being uttered by the reggae sound of Desmond Dekker. Jake entered a world of his own. Everyone in the room stood in stunned silence and watched him perform. For two minutes and thirty seconds he disappeared. He entered a state where there was no pressure to be anyone, he was free, he was equal; no, he was better than most at that one thing. He had a talent. He was brilliant.

Sam had never seen such rhythm since he'd watched his Uncle Winston 'perform' to a Bob Marley song at a family wedding back in Jamaica. Desmond's rendition ended as it had started, in stunned silence. Jake was returned to the real world, just as Sam led a slow applause which gained momentum as the whole hall joined in. It slowly dawned on Jake that this was for him, for something he had given without taking, he had provided pleasure and his reward was seeing the pleasure mirrored on other people's faces. They cheered and clapped as he left the dance floor.

His face turned as red as his socks and he moved to familiar territory near Fergie and Drip.

They, in turn, revelled in the reflected glory of Jake's cameo performance.

Paul mouthed across the room to Josh, 'Nice one son! ' Josh winked and raised a thumb in acknowledgement but immediately returned to the job in hand, as he now had the perennial DJ's problem of 'follow that':

The whole hall joined in as the chorus of his chosen response hit the speakers:

'Hi Ho silver lining!' exclaimed Jeff Beck and the room erupted in an explosion of laughter and dance. Even Jake and the boys joined in and the party had really started.

There was no trouble that night and as Josh put on the final record, Mary took her chance and grabbed Will's hand. She led him away from Sam and onto the dance floor for the first time that night.

Simon and Garfunkel were slowly enthusing about helping someone 'over troubled waters' as the two of them moved slowly round the floor. Mary held Will tightly and Will felt awkward. She rested her neck on his shoulder and pushed her lower body towards his. Will didn't quite know what he should do and simply moved round and round in a circle. Mary manoeuvred him to go in her direction as she moved her body close to his.

Suddenly Will relaxed as he felt a familiar stirring begin. He pushed back against Mary's movements and she smiled over his shoulder and shut her eyes as she too relaxed. Will gently lifted her head from his shoulders and looked into those beautiful eyes. He had never noticed how intensely blue they were before. She smiled back at him as the ' bridge was laying down' and he moved toward her lips with his own.

'Look at those two!' came a shout so loud that all eyes were diverted to the couple on the floor about to kiss.

'What are they up to?' continued Drip pointing toward Mary and Will. Jake stared at Will and all Will's previous fears returned in that one moment. Mary held on but knew the moment was wrecked.

'Let's go,' she said, 'Please take me home.'

The 'Bridge' was laid, and the full lights were switched on by Paul.

'Goodnight! Thanks for coming!' announced Josh, as Status Quo's 'Rollin' Home' played out as they cleared up.

Will and Mary left, completely ignoring Drip who continued his commentary to Jake and Fergie. Everyone else started leaving or helping with the clean-up.

Outside the hall Will and Mary stood and looked at each other.

'Can I walk you home?' asked Will, still feeling somewhat aroused from their recent close encounter.

'I'd like that,' replied Mary. 'Can we go through the park though,' she added.

Mary needed to go back to the 'little girl's room' before they left, as Will stood and waited by the door. Drip grinned as he walked past, Fergie completely ignored Will and Jake just looked at him with his stare. Will looked away.

Mary came back out, smiled at Will and declared, 'Let's go.'

They left the church hall and headed toward the park which would lead through to 'Mile End'. They could see the three boys ahead and hung back until they were out of sight. Will was worried about Sam, but Mary insisted that he was staying with Josh overnight. Will relaxed. They held hands and walked slowly toward the park.

It was an unusually mild evening for December, and they took forever to reach the park entrance. Of course, the gates were locked at that time and they would need to climb over the gates.

Will, being the true gentleman, went over first and beckoned Mary to follow. She reluctantly followed but as she dropped onto the ground Will was there to catch her. She landed facing him and looked longingly into his eyes as he stopped her from falling over. She moved closer and he placed his arms around her. They returned to their position on the dance floor and Mary pushed against his lower body.

She was prepared and knew exactly what was about to happen. Will didn't have a clue what was going on. He felt that same stirring below and this time their lips met without any childish interruption. Will melted into her mouth and their tongues fenced in a duel of ecstasy. Will felt himself grow and pushed himself harder against Mary. She in turn relaxed into him and was almost ready. Mary temporarily stopped and Will felt awkward in case he had upset her. She put one finger to her lips, stepped back from him removed her coat and laid it on the ground behind her. She sat down on the coat and signalled with a curled forefinger for Will to join her.

As he knelt forward, she unleashed his belt and freed him from his trouser prison. He moved forward and gently lay on top of her. Mary guided him as he entered her easily. She was so sure that this would be the night that she had already removed her underwear in preparation.

She smiled as Will succumbed to nature.

He reached up with his hand and encased her right breast under her jumper and as he caressed the soft bulge of flesh, he felt a growing sensation in the palm of his hand. He could not control himself and so quickly his lower body was consumed by an intense explosive feeling of pleasurable wetness and release. He let out a guttural sigh as he finally relaxed onto her body. Mary smiled inwardly and kissed the neck of her Will.

They lay together until the cold took over and eventually, they rose to their feet. Mary returned to full attire and they looked at each other and smiled. There was no embarrassment, everything was natural and as it should be.

'I love you, Will Brown, I always have.' said Mary as they left the park and entered the estate.

Will didn't really know what he felt, except good.

'I love you too, 'he felt obliged to reply, not really taking in what he was actually saying. They held hands until they reached her house and the goodnight kiss was much more intense than usual. Mary entered her house and turned to smile at Will before closing the door. Will waved, smiled as the door closed and decided to run home.

Chapter 26 ~ 1971

The letter arrived on cue. Will knew it was the one because he recognised the handwriting on the brown envelope. His own. He had stuck the stamp on it too and had handed it to his form master, at the King Edward grammar school, two months previously.

It contained his A-level results.

'Come on Will, hurry up and open it!' implored his Mother.

'Yes, put us out of our misery,' added his sister who had already torn apart her similar envelope as soon as it arrived. She had achieved her aim of two Bs and a C.

His Dad tried to keep out of it but eventually he could stand no more:

'Got to go now, Will,' hoping this would get the envelope opened. Will relented and tore the sealed edge. He carefully removed the small white results sheet; he slowly and deliberately unfolded it. He read the contents to himself, showing no emotion as the rest of the family watched anxiously. His face momentarily showed a frown for effect. He then immediately threw the paper in the air simultaneously bending both elbows and clenching his fists, whilst shouting, 'Yes, yes, yes, yes!'

He grabbed his Mum and gave her a big kiss as Susan bent to retrieve the abandoned paper.

It read,

'Biology:	A
Chemistry:	A
Mathematics:	A

An additional typed addendum declared:

Dr. Silas Marner prize for Biology:

William Brown for the essay 'The Study of Urban Lepidoptera'.'

It was signed underneath, in the usual school teacher's scrawl, 'Well done, Will. Doc. Marnie'

She screamed out the results to everyone and grabbed her brother before giving him a big kiss on each cheek.

'Well done Will,' said James shaking his younger brother's hand before giving him a man hug, which included the 'embarrassment-reducing' two pats on the back! James had completed his degree earlier that same year, gaining the expected First in 'Economics and Politics' and was already working full time with his father in the factory. In fact, he would be running the business for the next two weeks while the rest of the family went off to Spain for their annual break.

They had delayed this year's holiday as Will's results were due to arrive right in the middle of it. James had been to the villa during Factory Fortnight allowing his

Dad to take a full month off this year. John trusted James implicitly and anyway his own father would always be around to advise.

'Wonderful effort, Will' said John not bothering to worry about embarrassment as he cuddled his younger son tightly.

The Browns were a very happy family and now both twins were set for their respective universities. Will was to go to Durham to study Entomology, just as he had craved all his life.

Life seemed mapped out for Will.

Susan was off to study English, just like Mum, at Newcastle, near enough to Will 'just in case!' but with space between them.

Chapter 27

The letter arrived unannounced on the doormat of 56 Churchill Road. Mary picked up the brown, official looking envelope and handed it to her mum.

'What is it mum, a bill?' said Mary walking through to the kitchen and handing the letter to Carol.

'No idea, not expecting anything this week,' she replied as she finished her second cup of tea of the morning.

'We'd better be getting off to the shop, the papers will be arriving soon,' continued Carol, 'I'll take it with me and read it later.'

In truth she was worried about the contents.

It had happened two weeks previously:

The two of them had left home as usual at 5.30am to walk to the shop. They had to be there early to meet the paper delivery and get the bags ready for the boys to deliver the newspapers. Mornings in the shop were the busiest and 'the most profitable' as Cedric always reminded them. They arrived just as the delivery van pulled up; the driver smiled at Carol as he dumped the papers on the pavement and sped off up the road. Carol loved that smile.

Carol unlocked the front door of the shop and the two of them entered to begin their work as usual. Cedric had given her a key at the same time as he had decided to hand over the mornings to the girls, after the incident with Mary. He would still be in bed when they arrived and usually appeared after the morning rush with a welcome cup of tea at about ten. That morning had been especially busy, and it seemed never ending with one customer after another coming in.

They liked being busy but by 10.30, as peace descended, they were both looking forward to seeing Cedric appear with two cups of tea and a plate of fig rolls. He was convinced that everyone liked these biscuits as much he and Sheila had. They didn't notice his non-appearance for a while as they were still serving the occasional customer and tidying up the morning's chaos.

'I wish he'd hurry up, I'm gasping.' said Mary when the shop momentarily emptied.

'To be honest,' replied her mum 'I haven't heard a sound from upstairs. Let's give him another ten minutes,' she continued slightly concerned,' then I'll pop up.'

They carried on for a while with their work and still no movement or sound emanated from upstairs.

'Think I should nip upstairs?' offered Mary.

'No, I'll go, you carry on with sorting the sweets out,' said Carol somewhat more concerned now.

She went through the door behind the counter and nervously climbed the stairs. There was still no sound from Cedric's room. She reached the door and gently knocked. No response. She knocked several times with increasing force on each strike. No response. She turned the doorknob and pushed the door slowly into the bedroom. It was dark and a smell hit her nostrils immediately. She could see nothing at all and stumbled across to the window to pull back the curtains.

The light struck Cedric's blackened face as he lay unmoving in his bed.

She put her hand to her mouth and screamed. The scream brought Mary crashing up the stairs and into the room. She had never seen a dead person and simply cuddled her mum to shelter herself from reality. They stood together in shock before Carol ushered her distraught daughter through the bedroom door and back down the stairs to the comfort of the shop instructing her to put up the 'Closed' sign on the door.

A million selfish thoughts went through Carol's mind as she considered their future without the shop as she looked at Cedric.

'What will we do? How will we live? Where will we go?'

Practicalities interrupted her thought pattern; as Carol pulled the covers over Cedric's deep blue face. She opened the window and respectfully closed the curtains. She slowly and quietly shut the door as though she wanted to avoid waking him and went down the stairs.

'I'll phone the police and ambulance,' she told a sobbing Mary. It meant that she had to go outside to the public phone near the 'Green', as Cedric had never had a phone installed in the shop.

'Never needed one all my life, and can't see the need now,' she could almost hear him say.

Within minutes the shop was full. The police were the first to arrive, quickly followed by two jovial, ambulance crew. They immediately confirmed the obvious state of Cedric and, job done, they left as quickly as they arrived.

Sergeant Shelton was organisation personified as he

simultaneously calmed Carol and Mary and arranged for the local undertakers to carry out their duties. Cedric had already left written instructions for his own funeral with Mr. Hendry, of Hendry and Sons, Undertakers. He had done this just after his beloved Sheila had passed away, as at the time he never thought he would carry on living without her for very long.

'There is nothing for you to worry about,' Mr. Hendry said softly to Carol as the body was removed from the shop. 'We will carry out all of Cedric's requirements,' he continued.

'What should I do about the shop?' she enquired as though Mr. Hendry would know. 'I think you should carry on as usual for now, that's what he would have wanted.' 'But what about after that?' she asked herself.

The undertakers placed the body into their vehicle as a crowd gathered outside the shop. Carol and Mary returned to the shop and Sergeant Shelton closed the door behind them. 'There will have to be an inquest,' he informed Carol as she took a sip of her welcome cup of tea.

'Which will delay the funeral for a week or so,' he added. 'I suggest you close the shop for the rest of the day, but open tomorrow as usual Cedric wouldn't want his customers let down for too long.'

'I'll contact John Goodyear, Cedric's solicitor, as soon as I get back to the station. I'm sure he'll be in contact with you.' He said goodbye and departed.

The next two weeks passed in a bit of a haze as the 'Rodgers Girls' tried to carry on as usual in the shop. The inquest concluded that Cedric had died of heart failure; it had just had enough, it was finally broken. The funeral was simple and passed off without incident. Carol was amazed at the number of people who attended, to show their respects to an unassuming man. She shouldn't have been because, after all, he had served the local community for many years and although he was not a particularly sociable man, he had impeccable manners, in public at least, and was always polite. He was a popular shop keeper. He would be missed.

So, finally, after the usual busy morning Carol had the opportunity to open the brown envelope. She slowly tore across the edge of it and removed the neatly folded letter. It showed a letterhead which proudly announced: Goodyear and Goodyear, Commissioners of Oaths and Solicitors'.

It simply stated:

'Dear Mrs Rodgers,

You are formally invited to attend the reading of the last Will and Testament of Mr. Cedric Horatio Winston Smith. The reading will be held in the offices of the undersigned on Monday 30th August 1971 at 2.30pm.'

It was signed with the usual, solicitor's indecipherable scribble but underneath the scrawl, in legible typescript:

'J.G. Goodyear LL.B.'

Chapter 28

No letters were received in the Kirke's' household that morning.

Jake got himself ready for work as usual. Joe was on another 'sickie' as his back suddenly became too painful to get out of bed. Jenny couldn't be bothered to argue with him anymore and merely packed up Jake's sandwiches and placed them in his work bag. She would get out of the house today, as this was one of her mornings when she did housework for one of the residents on 'The Rise'.

A few months previously she had answered an advertisement, which had been placed in the window of the 'Sweet Shop'. It had been placed by Mrs Ashby, one of the teachers at St John's, who needed someone to clean her large house a couple of mornings a week. Mr. Ashby worked away a lot and in truth she was also looking for some company. Mrs Ashby, or Joan as she insisted on being called by a very nervous Jenny at the interview, took people at face value. She knew about Jenny's husband and her notorious son but looked into Jenny's eyes, noticing a fading bruise under one, and saw a spark of decency. She gave her a chance. Jenny loved being trusted and she returned the belief shown in her with hard work. She worked for Joan on Monday morning and the afternoons of Wednesday and Friday. The two women struck up an unlikely friendship during their afternoon chats as Joan arrived home to share a welcome cup of tea just before Jenny left. Every Friday afternoon Jenny would receive her cash, they agreed this would be beneficial to all, and she would leave with the customary:

'See you on Monday?' Joan was a lonely lady.

Jenny would deposit most of her weekly income into the savings account which she had secretly opened after taking the job. She kept a little back each week as a treat for Jake and sometimes for herself.

Joe must never know.

It wouldn't be just the extra money in Jenny's purse which would be of interest to Joe, although that would certainly come in handy down at the King's Head, it would be the potential information for his 'nocturnal' removal business' that he would knock out of Jenny. So for now, everyone was happy. Jenny had found a new lease of life and she had the feeling of being of value again. Jake received a regular treat as she enjoyed the look on his face whenever she presented him with the latest vinyl release. She saw how much the music meant to him. It was his private escape from Joe's influence.

Chapter 29

Carol and Mary sat nervously in the reception area of the offices of 'Goodyear and Goodyear'. They each surveyed the shelves filled with row upon row of leather-bound law books: ordered, labelled in gold leaf and, apparently, untouched. The bespectacled Miss Pilberry sat bolt upright at her desk typing at breakneck speed on her newly acquired electronic typewriter. She answered the disruptive ring of her green 'trim phone' with a polite authority and reassuring confidence, always making a note in the diary after replacing the handset.

They sat looking at the two imposing oak doors behind Miss Pilberry and at the shiny, respective name plates which adorned the wood: 'Mr. J.G. Goodyear LL.B' and 'Mrs J.P. Goodyear LL.B'. The girls sat together in silent awe.

At precisely 2.30pm the left side door squeaked open, and a kindly looking man of about sixty emerged with a pleasant welcoming smile on his reddish face. He walked straight over to the two women, who felt the need to adjust themselves as he approached.

He held out his hand to Carol and politely enquired: 'Mrs Rodgers, I presume?'

'Yes, and this is my daughter Mary, I hope you have no objections to my bringing her?' surprisingly confidently, replied Carol. The austere surroundings seemed to inspire her to a new level of self-belief.

'Not at all, I know how much Cedric thought of Mary and I believe what you are about to hear will affect her too.' said Mr. Goodyear pointing toward his opened door.

The room was as imposing as the outer office. There were two chairs already set out facing his large desk, which was completely clear except for a single sheet of paper, a fountain pen and a telephone. Not one of those new 'trendy shaped contraptions' but an old style, traditional telephone in keeping with Mr. J.G. Goodyear's standing. Behind him were more leather-bound tomes of law. He beckoned the two ladies to take a seat and he touched the back of Carol's chair as she sat, as any true gentleman would.

He sat down at his desk and made himself comfortable. He sensed their nervousness and put them at rest by giving them each a reassuring smile. They immediately relaxed.

'As you know, Cedric placed all his legal requirements in my hands, and it is my duty and pleasure to read his last will and testament to you.'

Carol suddenly, and for the first time, wondered why no one else was there to hear the reading.

Mr. Goodyear adjusted his 'pince-nez', lifted the piece of paper up, almost to his nose, and calmly read aloud from the script in front of him:

LAST WILL and TESTAMENT

This is the last Will and Testament of me Cedric Horatio Winston Smith born on 12th February 1901 of 3, The Parade, Mile End Estate, Northwich, made this 17th day of December 1970. I hereby revoke all former Wills and Codicils made by me and declare this to be my last will.

I appoint my solicitor John Goodyear to be the Executor of this Will

I devise and bequeath the residue of real and personal estate whatsoever to my companion Carol Rodgers

I wish my body to be buried

As witness my hand the day and year above written

C H W Smith

17th December 1970

Signed by the said testator in the presence of us at the same time who at his request and in his presence and in the presence of each other have subscribed our names as witnesses

First Witness:	Second Witness:
JG Goodyear	*GW Hendry*
J.G.Goodyear.	G.W.Hendry
8, The Close,	45 Rope St.
Northwhich.	Northwhich
Solicitor	Undertaker
17th December 1970.	17th December 1970

Carol and Mary sat in stunned silence, and looked at each other, as Mr. Goodyear removed the glasses from the end of his nose and placed the will on the desk in front of him. He smiled knowingly at the two people on the other side of his desk.

'What does that actually mean?' enquired Carol after several minutes of thought.

'It means that Cedric has left you everything he had, the business and his entire life savings,' matter of factly replied Mr. Goodyear.

He continued, after allowing the simpler explanation to sink in:

'I can't say exactly how much the savings are worth because there are still one or two bills to settle, including my own, but I would estimate the balance will be in the region of £30,000.'

Carol gasped.

'Of course, he has also left you the business, which as I am sure you will appreciate is an equally valuable asset. I will, if you wish, act for you to acquire the lease from the council to allow you to continue trading from the current premises,' continued Mr. Goodyear, returning to solicitor mode.

Neither of the girls spoke.

'I suggest you carry on as usual and I will arrange another meeting to discuss your requirements when this has all sunk in properly,' offered Mr. Goodyear.

They stood up in unison; each shook his hand and exited his office as he opened the oak door for them. They passed by Miss Pilberry, who carried on typing as if it was just another 'day in the life'.

Outside, the cool air brought both of them back to a sense of reality. Carol immediately grabbed her still shocked daughter and held her tightly.

'We are made for life, now,' she thought to herself as tears welled in her eyes.

Mary leaned on her mum's shoulder and thought she heard the door of the prison cell slam shut behind her.

Chapter 30

It was known locally as 'The Ravine' and rumour had long since concluded that it had been formed by a bomb!

In actual fact it was a natural pit, situated on the outskirts of the estates between them and the church. There was a surrounding sloping hillside which led down to the overgrown wasteland below. The local youngsters used the slope for tobogganing down during winter snow falls.

The pit had a dirt track leading down from the road which allowed access, but this was only rarely used and only ever by travellers. They sometimes arrived during summer months but after several run ins with locals, and in particular with Jake and his 'welcoming gang', they had not been seen for a while.

It was an area of trees, bushes, wild flowers and animals. Will loved going there and would sit for hours at the top of the hill, feet dangling over the edge just observing. That's why Mary suggested they meet there.

She could see him in position as she crossed the road from Mile End. He was miles away, in his own world when she touched his left shoulder and she sat down on his right. He instinctively looked to his left as she wiggled into position. He smiled, as he always did, at this little game of hers. She noticed his blond hair now curled up on his collar, and he looked so good with his unkempt locks and the tanned skin from his recent holiday.

The time had arrived.

'Hi ya, mate,' said Will coming out of his dreamworld. 'How's things?' he continued. 'Not bad,' she lied.

'Heard about the shop business being left to your mum, you must be well pleased,' 'A bit of a shock actually, but mum's delighted.'

They skirted around the real reason for their meeting for quite a while with small talk. Eventually Mary touched on the subject.

'I'm really going to miss you Will, when do you leave?' knowing full well, but somehow hoping he would decide that staying home was a better option than going to Durham University and then on to his dream.

'Tomorrow,' he casually replied, 'Dad's taking me and Susan up to the North East at the same time.

'Look at that,' he said, pointing to a rabbit scurrying through the wasteland below them. She couldn't focus on it through her welling eyes.

Will saw the tears and immediately placed his arm around her shoulder and she rested her head on his shoulder.

'I'll be home every holiday,' he said stroking her hair away from her wet face, 'and I'll be working in the factory and we can meet every day'.

'I know, but then we'll go through all this again,' she reasoned.

Will sensed that nothing he could say would change anything. He was going to go, he had to, it was his destiny, his dream since when he could remember.

He stood up and put out his hand to help her to her feet. She took it and raised herself to his eyelevel; they looked at each other longingly. She moved closer and they stood as one, kissing more passionately than they ever had before. Will broke the embrace and smiled as he moved away.

'I'll walk you home.'

'OK,' she reluctantly agreed.

They held hands and walked in silence all the way back to the estate. At the gate, they kissed each other gently and parted. As Mary approached her front door, Will pulled the gate shut and secured the bolt in place.

Mary thought she heard the key turn in her cell door.

Chapter 31

She entered the room with a mercurial grace. She seemed, as always, to be by herself and with everyone. The room was under her control. Will was quietly intrigued, her piercing eyes indicated she had noticed him. A seat at the bar appeared from nowhere and her usual drink was waiting. Drake, her ever-present companion, fussed around her as usual. Erica was everyone's dream. The boys fantasized about her and the girls all wanted to be her. She was stunning with her long dark, curly hair, she had the grace of a ballet dancer and she dressed like a gypsy queen. With a flick of her hair she swivelled to face the bar and the room continued.

Will sat and caressed his half-emptied glass as she made her entrance, alongside him were his two soul mates at university. They had been thrown together by fate and had met on that first day in the kitchen of their halls of residence at Durham University. Each had been delivered by an equally anxious set of parents who, after deliberate departure delaying tactics, had finally left them to start the next chapter of their lives.

'Let's go to the bar!' immediately declared the smallest of the three, Michael or 'Miguel' as he was affectionately known, due to his swarthy good looks and his particular love of Mexican food. It broke the awkward ice and they could sense the almost tangible release of their new-found freedom. They all immediately smiled and introduced themselves properly. It was the last time they felt nervous or embarrassed in each other's company.

They departed to the union bar, not for the last time, and never looked back. They were three 'amigos' almost by design.

Will was instantly elected leader of the group, the one they shared their problems with and the 'mug' lumbered with all the responsibilities, like the time he had had to explain to the housekeeper how the cooker got destroyed by a fire and the one lumbered with paying the bills on time. He was a natural and they loved him in different ways.

'Miguel' was the spark for almost all of their social life together, he thought life was for living and boy did he live it. He looked up to Will, in more ways than one, and would do anything for him. 'Miguel' was from the wrong side of town and his escape to university was his way out. He, like the other two, was a natural student and the expectations of university came easy. He was studying Law and would ultimately become a Barrister. It wasn't 'if' with 'Miguel', it was 'when'. No one argued with him for long, which was good preparation for his future career. He was small but his background had made him scared of nobody and absolutely nothing. He liked the girls and seemed to have at least three on the go at once and many a time Will had had to lie to one or other about his whereabouts. Will loved him like a brother and would, and did, do anything for him.

He was Will's surrogate Mary.

The other 'amigo' was a much more studious type who they quickly nicknamed 'Prof', for obvious reasons. Geoff, as he was actually christened, was from the right side of town and had sailed through everything, academically, that had been thrown at him. He too was studying Law and he shared a love of that subject with 'Miguel'. They argued all the time about points of law from the day's lectures, but of course 'Miguel' would never be defeated, and discussions could go on all night. They were like chalk and cheese, but each had a deep admiration for the other's inherent qualities. They spoke with different accents but thought in exactly the same way. Their passion was infectious. In fact, on many an occasion, during their vociferous debates, Will had seriously considered dropping his beloved subject and to take up Law!

'If they were ever to clash in court, as opposing barristers that would be a day to behold!' Will had thought to himself on many occasions.

Chapter 32

So, the pattern of university life was set for Will and his new-found buddies. They lived together, they studied together, they laughed together, they cried together, and they loved together. They would be true friends for life.

Both Prof and Miguel enjoyed the ladies and as far as the latter of the two was concerned, it was all a big game. He could never settle with 'building a relationship' and was only content with living on the edge. Will often mentioned the occasion when, one evening in their flat, he was forced to entertain one of Miguel's conquests over a drink in the lounge as Miguel was 'attending' to another in the bedroom. Will had had to make excuses and talk loudly for an hour. During Miguel's absence Will had taken two phone calls from other female friends waiting at various locations around the campus. Life was never dull with Miguel.

Prof, on the other hand, had met Sophia towards the end of the first year and the two had been inseparable since except, of course, when the 'amigos' called. Sophia was studying English and all she wanted to do was to teach her beloved subject. They were destined to be together for life. Will always thought about his own parents when Prof and Sophia were around. He, himself, only had eyes for Mary but knew other eyes were on him.

Will's life, at least for that first year, was an organised mixture of university life and going home for the holidays. He loved Mary, he missed her, and he remained as loyal as he could. There were always distractions.

He travelled home for Christmas that first year buzzing with excitement about his new life and was full of it when he met Mary that night on the anniversary of their first true encounter with love in the park.

'You must come to Durham and meet the boys,' said Will, 'You'd love them,' he added.

'I will,' she replied, knowing full well that she probably wouldn't. She would feel inadequate and show Will up, is how her mind worked. Will, as if reading the self-doubt, declared:

'They would all adore you Mary, I've told them so much about you, what you mean to me and our plans for the future,'

'I'll come next Spring,' was as committed as she could muster.

'That'll be wonderful,' excitedly replied Will as he moved towards Mary, and removed his beloved trench coat.

They lay down together on the sprawled coat under that same tree and repeated the wonderful loving act they had on that virgin occasion. This time it was less rushed and far more controlled than that previous encounter had been, borne from a distant separation and a deeper love and respect for each other. At the end they looked into each other's eyes and smiled. As so often, words were not needed between them.

The year passed and the pattern continued with the bond growing stronger with each encounter. Mary never made it to Durham next Spring.

Chapter 33 ~1972

The shop didn't normally provide a delivery service, but Mr. Cooke was an exception.

Mary had heard that he was unwell and therefore unable to make his weekly visit to collect one of his few remaining pleasures in life, his packet of 'Craven A'. Mary always coughed at the thought of the advertisement hoarding in the high street which declared: 'Craven A, will not affect your throat!'

Samuel J Cooke had been a regular visitor to the shop ever since Cedric opened it up in 1951 and every day he would arrive, by bicycle, to buy his pack of ten. When Mary and Carol took over the running, he was already an established customer. Nowadays, he didn't use his trusty old bike anymore and obviously struggled to make the long walk from his home. But whenever he made the effort to get to the shop, he always made the girls smile with some 'grumpy' observation, usually directed at 'today's youths' or the amount of litter left outside of the chip shop. As with most of his generation he had seen some active service in World War I and, as a part consequence, had developed a 'healthy' taste for 'ciggies'. The tobacco industry's contribution to the war effort had been to donate their product to a soldier's rations. Samuel's box had always contained 'The Black Cat' version of the cigarette.

After the war ended, Samuel had returned home and luckily found work on a local farm and, as part of the deal, lived in one of the two adjacent, tied cottages. The farmer, in time, decided that retirement was a better option than work and sold his land to the local council, who at that time were looking to build one of the new style council estates popping up all over the country. Samuel had taken some sound advice and had actually bought his cottage after his wife died. Their neighbours, Jack and Dora Etheridge, had lived next door for over twenty years now and since the passing of Jack, he and Dora looked out for each other.

It was Dora who mentioned to Mary that Samuel was not up to getting to the shop that week.

The two cottages are all that remain of the once thriving farm which had worked the sprawling, productive fields where now stood the 'Mild End' and 'The Rise' estates. A busy road separates Samuel and Dora's life from other human contact and the outlook from their respective windows is of the flat roofed, dark bricked imposing building with the huge sign proudly announcing: 'Brown's Cardboard'. Samuel and Dora are so proud of their continued independence and whenever asked how she is Dora's standard reply is always, 'Mustn't grumble'.

Dora would still make her stick-aided stroll to the grocery shop every day and Samuel would usually accompany her on a Friday to call into 'Cedric's' for his 'ciggies'. He couldn't get used to girls running a tobacco shop and he certainly wouldn't call it by the new name 'C & M's'! It was, and always would be, 'Cedric's' to him.

So, after hearing about Mr. Cooke's illness, Mary had decided to personally visit him with his weekly supply together with a few other luxuries like a piece of Madeira cake her Nan had left the day before. It was her lunch break and, anyway, the walk would do her good. She also knew that Rory, the newspaper delivery man, would call in at the shop on his way home from work. Carol would be happy for the rest of the day!

As Mary passed the huge wrought iron gates of the factory, she saw there was some sort of a commotion on the main road, just opposite the two cottages. She anxiously pushed her way through to join the throng of nosey, gathering bodies at the kerb side. The first thing she saw was an upturned wicker, shopping basket in the middle of the road and its spilled contents nearby comprising a red leather purse, a single carrot, two small potatoes and a tin of 'Fray Bentos' corned beef. A lonely, loose toilet roll had unravelled itself forming a curled white pathway across the road before coming to a halt at the kerb.

In the middle of the road was Mrs Etheridge being very cautiously helped to her feet by a tall, well built, young man. He was gently helping her to her feet and simultaneously collecting her belongings to return to her bag. He handed her the walking stick she had dropped and supported her arm, as he helped her very slowly to move towards the safety of her home. The young man glared silently, but with some menace, toward the driver of a grey mini-van, whose journey had come to an abrupt halt at the feet of the old lady. The driver acknowledged the glare with an embarrassed downward glance. The young man took all the time Mrs Etheridge needed to reach her destination on the other side of the road. He gentlemanly opened the creaky wooden gate to her property and walked her down the overgrown path to the wooden front door of 'Primrose Cottage'. He opened the unlocked door for her and helped her inside. He accompanied her in and closed the door behind him.

'What happened?' Mary asked as an open question to any of the remaining crowd.

'I think the old dear tripped up as she crossed the road,' replied an anonymous bystander. 'She fell right in front of the mini-van,' said another.

'The big lad came running from nowhere to stop the traffic and help her.' Someone else chipped in before moving away with most of the crowd, who'd had their fill.

Soon there was just Mary and one other on the kerb watching the traffic flowing normally again after its brief interruption.

'He was so good and wouldn't let her attempt to get up until he was happy she was okay,' said Mary's company.

'He was so kind and makes you think that not all 'that sort' should be tarred with the same brush,' she added.

'That sort?' Mary considered as her company departed. Mary continued her own journey and crossed the road towards Mr. Cooke's cottage. She opened the door and shouted up the stairs.

'Only me!', 'Mary from Cedric's,' she continued, knowing the mere mention of 'Cedric's' would reassure him.

'How are you feeling?' Mary enquired, still shouting up the stairs.

'On the mend, I'll be back in the shop next week, thank you,' returned Samuel. Mary left the cigarettes and cake on the kitchen table.

'OK, I'll be off then,' Mary replied, as she opened the front door.

As she exited the door and momentarily hovered behind the overgrown laurel bush, which straddled the boundary of the two properties, she saw the young man walk down the pathway from Mrs Etheridge's, open the gate and turn to close the gate. As he turned without looking up, she recognised him immediately in his Harrington and boots. One of 'that sort'.

It was Jake.

Chapter 34

Mary was topping up the Lemon Bon Bons into one of the many glass jars that adorned the shelves of the shop when the image of Jake, gently helping a little old lady to her feet, came into her head. She smiled at the thought and wondered.

'Don't forget I need the till contents when you've finished with the sweets,' Mary's mum demanded as Mary momentarily removed the picture from the cinema in her head.

'You know how long it takes me to count those new-fangled coins and fill in the paperwork,' she continued.

'Whose bright idea was it, anyway, to change from two hundred and forty pennies to the pound to just one hundred? It used to be so simple!' she mumbled to no one in particular.

Mary had heard this every Tuesday since February last year, and simply raised her eyebrows toward the sky and smiled again. She was feeling a bit happier today after witnessing Jake's 'Good Samaritan' act. She had been a bit down recently because Will had been away for what had seemed an age and she was missing him so much. Had he found someone more exciting? Was he tiring of her? Was he getting bored with her perceived 'inconsequential' self? These, together with a thousand other questions of doubt, had been rumbling through her mind? He'd cited having to do more work this year as a reason for not being able to get home for every holiday. The 'seeds of self-doubt', ever present in her mind, were being watered.

Carol had taken responsibility for the money side of the business since they inherited the shop from Cedric. Despite her mumblings she was very meticulous with the accounts, exactly how Cedric had taught her.

'Look after the pennies and the pounds will look after themselves,' he quoted to her ad nauseum during those sessions poring over the books.

'He'd have to say 'pence' now,' Carol often thought to herself. 'What would he have made of decimalisation?' she added, knowingly, to her thought process.

And so, every Tuesday she removed the bags of coins and notes from the shop's safe and, together with the day's till contents, she'd double check the money and enter the details onto the deposit slip ready to accompany the cash to the bank. The little plastic bags of money would be placed in the large yellow, cloth bag provided by Lloyds Bank and returned to her safe overnight before being taken to the bank. Carol often thought to herself, in jest, that the word 'Swag' should be printed in large, black print on the outside of the bag!

Cedric had always said, 'Lloyds Bank was the only proper bank you could trust.' Carol could see no good reason to change and carried on using 'The Black Horse' for all the shop's banking needs. This, however, meant that someone had to carry the yellow bag of 'Swag' to the bank in town every week.

It had become Mary's job to transport the sometimes very heavy yellow bag to the Lloyds branch in the town every Wednesday evening after work. She would place the bag into her straw shopping basket and cover it with a cardigan. She had to catch the bus from the top of the road and journey to town. She always felt vulnerable until the yellow bag was safely deposited into the jaws of the 'Night Deposit' safe bricked into the secure wall of the bank. They couldn't afford for Mary to be away from the shop during the bank's opening times and this was the next best option. Mary's 'reward' was to call into one of the new bars in town and meet an old school friend for a catch up. She had different plans for tomorrow's trip.

The following morning the shop was busy, as usual, with customers picking up their daily papers, their smokes, their snacks and the two of them were rushed off their feet. Mary, however, was going to find time for him on this particular morning.

So, when Jake arrived at 7.30 to pick up his copy of 'The Sun', Mary casually approached him at the paper rack on the far side of the shop. She carried a pile of newspapers in the pretence of replenishing stocks.

'Morning Jake,' she said sliding a few copies of 'The Daily Mirror' into position on the rack.

Jake was miles away, he hadn't even glanced at the headline that day: 'Massacre at the Games', after all he was only interested in 'Page 3'. As usual, he tucked the folded paper under his arm and turned toward the counter with his 3 pence ready in hand when she had spoken.

'Oh, hello Mary,' he replied in surprise at her close proximity. 'What are you doing tonight?' she said somewhat bravely.

'Probably meeting the boys and going to the pub later,' was his stock reply to any arrangement of social events in his life.

'You mean with Drip and Fergie?' asked Mary.

She had become increasingly weary of the, hitherto, quiet Drip ever since that day he came into the shop on his own. It was a very hot day and Mary had taken off her pale green, cotton work coat when he nervously entered through the opened door of the shop and through the hanging, multi-coloured fly screen. He got caught up in the long plastic strips she recalled with a smile. Mary admitted to herself later that her blouse was a bit revealing especially when she bent forward. Drip approached the counter and Mary greeted him with a pleasant smile.

'Hello, how can I help? She asked.

'I... I'd like a packet of those please,' he replied, pointing to the packets of 'Wrigley's' chewing gum in a box positioned toward the front of the counter.

Mary had had to reach across the counter to the box and as she did, gravity took over the control of her ample bosom and more than she was comfortable with was suddenly available for public consumption. She could feel Drip's eyes piercing her squashed cleavage and immediately stood up and rearranged her top. Drip bowed his head as a line of yellow effluent departed from the nose on his now reddened face. He paid Mary the two pence for his purchase without raising his head, turned and made a bolt for the door. After another fight with the fly screen, he sprinted away.

Mary felt intruded upon and immediately put on her working coat. She had always seen Drip as a sidekick, he did things for Jake and in return he received security from Jake. Mary had always felt uncomfortable in his presence mainly due to the way he looked at her, and in particular, her breasts.

After this incident she told herself that he was, after all, a developed man and following her previous experience with the 'gentlemanly' Cedric, she should have learnt her lesson!

'Well how do fancy coming into town with me tonight?' she continued questioning the still surprised Jake.

'I have an errand to do for the shop and I'd like you to accompany me,' she continued.

With her reformed opinion of Jake and the fact that he would be good secure company on the trip to the bank, she was hoping he would say yes.

The request was a shock to Jake after so many past rebuffs and, notwithstanding, the omnipresence of Will, he was unsure how to answer and felt there must be an underlying reason.

'You mean, like on a date?' he hopefully asked.

'Well, sort of,' she replied 'More of a trip to town, a drink after the errand and take it from there kind of a date.'

Jake would take anything that involved Mary without 'the long-haired lover from Durham'. 'What errand are you on?' enquired Jake, still intrigued.

Mary had always given Jake the benefit of doubt in his, sometimes, errant behaviour. The recent event with Mrs Etheridge had confirmed that she had been right to do so. She felt now that she could introduce the word 'trust' into her thoughts of Jake.

'I have to take the shop's weekly takings to the bank in town, and I'd very much like you to accompany me,' said Mary.

Jake was taken aback. This seemed too good to be true and he was elated to be able to go 'out' with Mary. Nothing would make him say no.

'Yes,' he answered, 'What time do you want me here?'

They sat together, upstairs, on the 18.16 double decker bus from the 'Parade' heading for town. Mary's stocking encased thigh bounced alongside Jake's 'Levi's' as the bus jogged and bumped its way out of the estate toward the main road and on into town. Mary didn't attempt to move her leg and Jake certainly wasn't going to.

They travelled in comfortable silence until they reached the bus station.

'This is it,' said Mary and they climbed slowly down the metal stairs and alighted the bus.

'We have to go to Lloyds around the corner and then we can go to 'The Prince of Wales' opposite,' continued Mary as they walked past the station's ticket office.

'I thought the bank closed at three,' Jake asked, not quite understanding.

'It does,' Mary answered with a slight grin, 'I use the 'Night Safe' for deposits,' she continued.

This was unchartered territory for Jake, being more interested in bank 'withdrawals' than deposits.

He watched with intense interest as Mary pulled open the handled front of the 'Night Safe' from the metal container in the wall of the bank. She lifted the cardigan in her basket and removed the heavy yellow bag with some effort.

'Do you want me to help? Jake offered.

'Yes please,' said Mary as she handed over the bag of 'Swag' to the newly entrusted Jake. 'Now what? he asked, still a bit unsure of the process.

'Place it in here,' she said indicating the now exposed 'hole in the wall'. Jake dropped the bag with ease into the void and Mary returned the handled front, back and flush with the wall. A resounding clunk was all the relief she needed to hear.

Still a little confused, with a hint of interest for future reference, Jake asked. 'So, if you open the box again is your bag still sitting there?'

'Of course not, it drops down into the bank as soon as the door is shut,' she answered with another grin. 'Look,' she continued offering him a demonstration. The penny had dropped!

Ten minutes later they sat side by side in 'The Prince of Wales'. Jake had a pint of Tartan in front of him as Mary sipped at a glass of dry cider. A 'ska' tune was playing on the juke box and Jake happily mouthed along to the incomprehensible words of the song.

'Would you like to do this again next week?' Mary asked.

Jake took a large mouthful of his beer before he replied, 'What, like a second date?'

Mary smiled thinking of her new-found trust and replied, 'Let's wait and see'. She wasn't going to rush this, whatever this was.

Jake couldn't be happier. A second date with Mary, no Will in sight and some valuable information filed away inside his not so skin head.

Chapter 35

Mary sensed something creeping up behind her for a while before it happened.

It was the end of the summer holidays and Will had just returned to university for his second year, after what seemed an eternity of lazy, loving days together. Of course, she had had to work in the shop and Will, as usual, had gone on his annual Spanish jaunt with his close-knit family. How Mary wished the Browns would allow her into their sanctum and she could have gone too. But, as always, Mary relished the moment and drank in the time alone with Will. Life seemed to have other plans for Mary: the shop, mum, routine and Jake. All safe and secure, no danger, no edge, no me and no dreams.

He'd always come second, third or even fourth. Never first choice for anything in his life. He was the fourth boy in the family, which craved a girl and ended up with him. He was the skivvy of the family and got all the jobs nobody else wanted. He got all the hand-me - downs and had never received a brand new anything in his entire life. His only 'friend' was another 'Billy no- mates' who, somehow, happened to have 'got in' with the class bully. He had therefore only joined that gang by default and did so because he wanted to feel part of something, anything which would give him a reason to bother about his perceived meaningless life. Nobody knew, or cared, that he had thoughts, he had opinions, he had feelings, he even had his own dreams and he was someone. Nobody took the trouble to see him. He'd always had a 'thing' for Mary. She was perfection personified to him, never demanding, always accepting and she was the most outwardly and inwardly beautiful person he knew. She was never dismissive of him and she always tried to let him present his point of view before Jake gave it for him. He would never stand a chance with Mary who, he knew, only had eyes for Will. He had noticed Jake worming himself much closer to her after Will went off to uni. When Will started to stay away for longer periods he had seen Jake get even closer, or so he thought.

So, after years of festering frustration with his designated position in life, not to mention the sudden dramatic changes in his body, the frustration had turned to burning resentment, anger, despair and an aching need. He wanted more, even he deserved something more and he was going to get it. If he couldn't have it, he was going to take it!

Mary was returning home after a night out with a couple of ex school friends. They had spent a few hours catching up over drinks in the 'Kings Head'. Unusually, Jake and the gang were conspicuous by their absence in the pub that night. A bat hovered above her head as dusk was just settling over the park. She passed by the pond, where she had spent so many hours with Will simply sitting on the bench close by. There was nobody else about and it was eerily quiet and peaceful as her thoughts, once again, turned to those times with Will.

She thought she'd heard a twig crack behind her, but her mind was still on her favourite subject and she carried on with her leisurely walk home. Another shuffle from behind which, rousing her from her thoughts, sounded like the noise of a boot on gravel. This time she erased her thoughts, returned to real life and slowly, nervously turned her head to look behind. Nothing. 'Come on Mary, get a grip,' she thought to herself but none the less, she quickened her stride and allowed 'Will' to evaporate from her thoughts so she could concentrate on the now.

He'd seen her slow her stride and as she turned to look, he had skipped behind the large Willow tree, resplendent with its magnificent drapes of yellow leaves over-hanging the still pond. His heart was pounding far more than normal, and his temple was throbbing without control. He wanted to run away as fast as he could in the opposite direction to his target. Then his mind's eye caught sight of all those faces of people laughing at him, telling him what to do, what to think and putting him in his place at the bottom of the pile. An animalistic urge of confidence pulsed through him, this was his time. He adjusted the black Balaclava over his head and made sure the nose hole allowed access to fresh air. He needed that. His wild eyes peered through the slits of his headgear. Before the urge abated, he sprinted toward his target and in a few paces, he could see the whites of Mary's eyes as he knocked her onto the soft grass. She fell, conveniently, on her back. He immediately sat astride her prone body and muffled her screams with a gloved hand over her mouth. He was unsure what to do next, but the 'animal' directed his other hand to her left breast. He squeezed so hard that Mary let out a muffled scream and she simultaneously bit his hand.

He instinctively removed both hands and felt the need to raise his body into a kneeling position to relieve the growing ache between his legs.

Mary took her chance. As he rose momentarily from her trapped body, she flexed the strong muscle in her right thigh to deliver her leg to its vulnerable target. In one movement she'd bent it upwards and brought her knee joint, with a thrusting force, into the softest, most sensitive and temporarily aroused part of his anatomy. She had kneed him in the 'balls'.

He screamed in agony. He immediately lifted himself completely from her and as he rose a small drop of snot slid from the Balaclava's nose hole and landed on Mary's cheek producing a cold, slimy sensation. He jumped up, clutching at his pain and gave it a quick count and simultaneous rub. He ran as fast he could away from that surreal, nightmarish scene and well into the darkness of the night. She would never see him again.

In that moment Mary knew and he knew she'd know.

Mary stood up and brushed herself down. She looked around and felt isolated, violated but somehow understood. She felt nothing but pity for him. That was typical Mary.

She decided to go home and sleep on it.

Chapter 36 ~ 1973

Tuesday night was always 'catch up' time for the students, as it was too removed from last weekend, and not on the slope down towards the next one, to be a night to go to the bar.

'Perfect night then,' thought Will, as he finished counting the words of the penultimate dissertation for his degree, 'to go for a quiet beer.'

He'd worked solidly for a week on this latest piece of work: 'The Mutualism Relationships of the Butterfly' and the only worry was the number of words he'd finally managed to compromise on. Will's biggest problem with his work was his love of the subject and being unable to keep below the maximum word limit. His passion ran away with any restrictions and he 'rambled on', or so said his mentor the eminent Professor Theo Jackson. This time he had been restricted to nine thousand words and he'd just counted eight thousand six hundred and ninety-four! He prayed he'd counted correctly.

Will loved nothing more than a good night in the union bar, especially with Miguel and the 'Prof', when all the world's problems were solved over a beer or two and life seemed to be for the living. He sometimes felt guilty whenever he was having such a good time knowing that Mary was at home patiently awaiting his returns. These returns had become less frequent as his workload intensified, but he would make it all up to her eventually he had convinced himself. Meanwhile, he relished the company, the freedom, the beers and, of course, the sight of Erica.

Will had always been intrigued by 'The Gypsy Queen', as she had been quickly nicknamed by the boys. She was considered an unobtainable flirt as she always arrived with Drake but always seemed to be on her own. It wasn't as if none of the boys hadn't tried to chat her up, but nobody ever left the bar with her, except Drake. It was assumed he was her boyfriend.

Will had always acknowledged her and he sensed a deeper person than the exterior portrayed, but he couldn't be bothered to make any effort to seek favour. If she wanted to be aloof, then that was her choice. He still could not help feeling a basic, magnetic attraction towards her. Those beautiful eyes always seemed to seek him out.

As he clipped the final sheet of typed A4 into his ring file ready for tomorrow's presentation of his dissertation, he told himself again that he had earned that quiet drink. The boys were hard at work on their final respective pieces and the only sound from their rooms was the click, click of a typewriter. They each had a different 'Bar' on their minds tonight.

Will left the flat and headed along the road and back toward the university building a short distance from where they had been living for the last twelve months. He entered the union bar to the sound of 'See Emily Play'.

'Is that the only track they ever play in here?' he thought as he entered the almost deserted bar.

Will saw it was Jason on duty and guessed it was him who was so in love with 'Emily'. Jason approached from the opposite side of the counter as Will came in sight.

'Hi Will, usual?' asked Jason, using both of his hands to simultaneously part his long, straight, black hair, like a pair of curtains being drawn, to reveal his face.

'Yes please,' answered Will. 'Busy in here?' he sarcastically enquired with a grin.

'Tuesday mate, catch up night,' replied Jason, placing Will's pint of lager and lime on the counter. Will still didn't really like lager and only found it palatable with a dash of lime. He wondered with each pint he drunk what Jake would have to say about that! He didn't care.

'Is it?' Will's sarcasm continued. Jason smiled, took the ten pence offered to him by Will and threw it into the till. He rewound the tape on the bar's cassette player and pushed 'play' for 'Emily, to try it another way'.

Will picked up his pint and wondered to himself where to sit. He even played the sarcasm card to himself!

Then he saw her.

Even from the back view he knew who she was with that long, black curly hair and the flow of her dress somewhat crumpled as she sat nursing a small glass containing a murky liquid.

In a brave moment a few months earlier, and after he had had a few pints of Dutch courage, Will had offered to buy her a drink. Expecting a rebuff, she had surprisingly smiled directly at him and replied:

'Pernod and ice, please'.

He had never bought one of those and complained when it went cloudy as the ice was tipped in. It fitted her perceived persona perfectly.

'Hello Erica,' he confidently said as he pulled back the adjacent chair, 'This is the only seat available,' he continued with his sarcastic theme. She didn't bother to answer.

She sat in silence playing with her glass, swilling the remaining contents around its sides. Will caught the characteristic odour of aniseed.

'Can I get you another one?' asked Will, praying she'd say no as his current cash flow was at its limit until his allowance came in.

Without looking up and still continuing to swirl the glass and contents she politely replied, 'No thanks,' Will silently puffed his lips out.

A folded broadsheet newspaper lay on the table in front of her and Will reached forward to pick it up. Her hand slammed down on the paper before Will could actually touch it. She looked up for the first time to tell him to leave the paper exactly where it was.

He had always loved her dark brown, beautiful eyes which had stared invitingly at him so many times from across the room. This time they were red and blurry. She had been crying and, judging by the trail of dried salt down both cheeks, for some time too.

'What was that white stain just under her nose,' he questioned himself.

He didn't know what to say or do, Erica controlled

everything around her, or so he had always thought. She was in charge, what could possibly upset her so much. It suddenly dawned on him that she was alone. Where is Drake? he thought to himself.

'Where's Drake?' he eventually decided to ask.

She put the glass down and immediately burst into tears. This time he did know what to do and his arm went around her as she turned and buried her face into the area between his neck and shoulder blade. She shuddered as she sobbed. Will stroked her hair and sat with her in silence until the sobbing and shuddering of her body subsided and finally stopped.

Will didn't notice when he appeared silently behind them. He sat on the other side of Erica and the scraping of the chair roused her from Will's comfort pad. She wiped her eyes and momentarily concentrated on the intruder. He simply picked up the folded newspaper on the table, of which she had been so protective minutes before, and replaced it with an identical, similarly folded paper. He nodded knowingly to Erica, stood up and departed as silently as he had arrived. Erica place her hand on the new delivery and returned her head to its previous safe cradle near Will. Will replaced his comforting arm and waited for her to respond to his still hovering question.

Eventually she sat up and using a tissue, extracted with some difficulty from her dress pocket, blew her nose and wiped those brown eyes. She moved the newspaper and placed it under her bottom. Will thought he saw a corner of a transparent plastic bag as she moved the paper. Probably just the TV magazine he innocently thought to himself.

'Sorry, what did you say?' she eventually asked after composing herself. Will repeated his question concerning the whereabouts of Drake.

'He's had to go home,' she replied as the tears welled again.

Will was not worldly wise but even he knew that there was a story that needed to be shared and she wanted to share it with someone. He was that someone.

'Why has he had to go?' said Will.

'To see our mother,' she answered waiting to see the reaction on his face. 'Your MOTHER!' was Will's astonished reaction.

'Well actually his stepmother and my mother,' she further explained as she blew her nose on the now very soggy tissue. At that moment Will wished he had that clean handkerchief with him that his mum had told him always to carry.

Erica then blurted out the full story, interrupted only by her stopping occasionally to wipe the tears from her eyes.

'Mum married Donnie a couple of years after Dad died. Donnie had a son, Malcolm, and the four of us lived together in our new house,' she explained.

'Malcolm?' asked, a somewhat confused Will.

'Yes, that's Drake's actual name, he didn't think it was 'sexy' enough to be around uni with a name like Malcolm, so he changed it to Drake to give himself an air of mystery,' she further explained.

'Intriguing was dead right,' Will thought to himself.

'Anyway, all was good for a few months then it started,' she continued.

'Donnie started getting violent towards Malcolm and every morning he would have a different bruise or cut somewhere on his body, which Malcolm always found an excuse for. I knew he was being abused and confronted Donnie about it one day. He didn't take too kindly to me interfering in his business and so he started on me. Subtly at first and then eventually he would come into my room at night and *hurt* me. Neither me nor Malcolm dared to tell mum in case he started on her.'

Will was getting more uncomfortable as the story unfolded but squeezed her hand as she went on.

'I became very close to Malcolm and we decided that as soon as I started uni that he would come away with me and we would share a flat. I would attend classes and he could get a job locally. He would turn up at the uni in the evenings to protect me. We shared our flat with Gaynor and life was really good. Then, two days ago, we got a call from Mum to say he had started on her and that's where Malcolm is now.'

Will was speechless, this was as far removed from his family life as you could get. He felt obliged to say something.

'Have you heard from Malcolm?'

'Yes, Mum is staying with her sister and Donnie has been reported to the police. She is fine for the moment.' answered Erica somewhat relieved to have finally shared her burden with someone.

Her eyes had returned to their beautiful, natural brown as she turned toward Will and very gently kissed him on his cheek.

'Thank you for listening,' she whispered in his ear.

She stood and retrieved the newspaper she had been sitting on. Will noticed how careful she was not to let the paper unravel! She kissed him on the other cheek and asked, 'Can we meet again?'

'Of course,' replied Will,' Let's make Tuesday our date night in here.'

'Deal,' she said, holding a finger over her nose as she squashed a nostril and sniffed up strongly. She flicked her long curling hair over her shoulders and as graceful as ever was gone.

Will didn't move for an hour, it was a lot for him to take in. All he knew for sure was that he'd never again 'judge a book by its cover' and would always seek one fact more!

'Emily' was still being 'played'.

Chapter 37

'The army, the fucking army!' Jake's voice boomed all around the King's Head, momentarily drowning the sound of 'The Stones' enjoying some 'Brown Sugar' on the jukebox.

'The fucking army!' he repeated, as if to convince himself that what he'd heard was real. Jake had, as usual, been ruling the roost that lunchtime when Fergie nervously announced that he, and Drip, had been to the 'Army Recruiting Office' and had decided to sign up. Drip was very quiet.

'Why didn't you tell me?' said Jake, slightly calmer now that he realised that he had heard correctly.

'Because we knew how you'd go off!' somewhat confidently replied Fergie.

'When are you leaving?' said Jake in the hope that it was not for some time and they'd change their minds. He didn't fancy being left alone.

'Next week,' was the curt reply.

'Next fucking week,' again screamed Jake, once more interrupting 'Mick' and his 'Cajun Queen'. 'Why the fucking army?' he continued.

Trevor, the owner of the King's Head had heard enough. He calmly excused himself from his customer, lifted the bar hatch and secured it on its hook. He wiped his beer-soaked hands on his favourite tea towel and made his way to the table where Jake, and his, hitherto loyal, disciples sat. He merely stood over Jake and looked at him. Jake was silent immediately.

Trevor was a book you certainly didn't judge on the chapter you walked in on! Jake and Trevor had previous. Together they had worked out a mutual, working relationship, whereby Trevor knew he could rely on Jake to help in the removal of unwanted clients from his pub and, in return, Jake was not banned from the pub because of a previous incident.

In a previous life Trevor had been a member of the 'Paras'. On the very rare occasions that he rolled his left shirt sleeve high up his well-toned arm in anger, the famous 'Crowned and Winged parachute' of the regiment was revealed by tattoo, to confirm his membership of that famous regiment. He had served in Tunisia during the Second World War and in 1942 had been awarded 'The Military Medal' for bravery. The medal was now displayed on a shelf behind the bar, sandwiched between the dart trophy and a long-forgotten Sunday Football Cup.

Trevor only took the medal down once a year to wear when he attended the 'Remembrance Day Service' at St. John's Church on the estate. It would be returned to the shelf after the service and only referred to if ever asked about. He never mentioned those days. Trevor wanted simply to run his public house and to see people enjoy life, at least for the time they were in the 'King's Head'. However, he was protective and sensitive about the army, and nobody, but nobody, bad mouthed it in his presence. Trevor was usually the genial host of his domain, where hard working, ordinary people could relieve themselves of their problems and be free from the drudgery of their working week. He hadn't become successful in this trade, on that tough estate, without being able to look after himself, his property and his clients. He was well-aware of the explosive cocktail of alcohol and testosterone. So was Jake since that day:

It was a Saturday lunchtime sometime just after Jake had become a more frequent legal, partaker of a pint. Of course, for several years before that Jake had been brought to the 'Kings Head' by his dad. Joe would give Jake a coke and a packet of 'Smith's' crisps outside in the beer garden, where he would patiently play on the swings and wait for his dad to have his fill. On this particular afternoon, Jake was feeling down after a particularly stressful week in the factory. A few pints of 'Tartan' had put things into perspective. The 'cocktail' was brewing when they entered the pub. Two errant football supporters wearing the 'Claret and Blue' of West Ham. They were looking for no more than a pre-match drink. Jake was looking.

Jake, now, preferred playing local football rather than going to the 'Big Match'. After all, no one watched the game on the pitch, it was all about the 'game' off the pitch and trouble.

Jake and his ilk had inserted the word 'hooligan' into football. Of course, he used to be up there with the 'best of them' and felt elation when his firm came out on top. He rarely knew the score of the game. One day he lost. He was walking home this particular Saturday evening after an eventful match and encountered a dozen of the 'Inter City Firm'. He was on his own and had been ambushed. Jake could look after himself, but the numbers were not in his favour and he stood his ground until sense dictated he should run. Despite his size, he was pretty fit from his football training and he managed to lose the following posse. He had been really scared for the first time in his life and vowed never to go back. Those 'Claret and Blue' colours, however, burned him inside with hatred.

So, there they were, two laughing 'gnomes' wearing those colours, in his pub. Excuse enough, Jake thought to himself. They had each ordered a drink and exchanged some banter with Trevor before moving past Jake's stool at the bar. As the first one went past, Jake casually lifted his elbow to nudge his filled glass. Immediately the beer cascaded down his scarf, onto his black 'Sta-Prest' and eventually drenched his recently polished 'bovver' boots.

'Watch what you're fucking doing mate,' he said looking down at Jake, still casually sitting on his stool. Jake rose to his feet and well above his enemy. 'Or fucking what?' reasoned Jake. The other gnome came to support his mate and stared into Jake's eyes with a menacing look. Wrong thing to do! Jake immediately welcomed him to the 'King's Head' with one of his famous 'kisses'. The gnome dropped his pint with a satisfying, filled-glass explosion onto the floor, clutched his bleeding, broken nose and made a smart move toward the door.

The other gnome stood immobilised, not quite knowing what to do next and still clutching his untasted, half-filled glass of beer. Jake waited for the next move. Trevor didn't. Just like his regiment's motto: 'Utrinque Paratus', he was ready. He left the bar as Jake's head butt hit his man and in one lightening move landed a single punch onto Jake's face.

Jake went down like the proverbial 'sack' and fell onto the beer-soaked floor as Trevor directed the remaining gnome to join his mate and go now! Later, Jake recalled that his only memory of the incident was of a super-fast 'Winged Parachute' coming in his direction! He assumed this was a memory distortion caused by the punch. When the gnomes had exited through the door and ran off down the road, Trevor threw the contents of the ice bucket onto Jake still laying prostrate on the floor. His 'Fred Perry' now as wet as his fellow gnome's 'Sta-Prest'. He came to and shook his throbbing head, reluctantly feeling around the bruise just under his left eye. 'What the fuck happened?' he groggily asked one of the other stunned customers. 'Trevor happened,' was the reply. 'Think yourself lucky, he could have killed you!' he continued. Trevor had, by now, returned to his duties behind the bar, as though nothing had happened, and was deep in conversation with another customer. It suddenly dawned on Jake that he had been put in place by a chapter he had never even read, and 'respect' suddenly entered his limited vocabulary.

So, when Trevor appeared at the table to oversee the 'army' discussion with Fergie and Drip, Jake already knew his place. Trevor didn't have to say a word, he merely gave Jake his own stare and Jake was sorted.

'We go to Catterick for fourteen weeks 'Basic Training,' continued Fergie. Drip was still keeping quiet. 'Then the army decides where we go next,' he added, just in case Jake thought that they would be back then.

'There's nothing for us here except this,' he said eyeing around the room with hands splaying outward. 'We want something better'.

'What about me?' questioned Jake feeling more isolated, as the conversation continued. 'What am I going to do?'

'Your problem, mate,' thought Fergie. 'Mary's my

only hope,' thought Jake.

Drip didn't think, perfect for the army. He just knew he had to 'get out of town'.

Chapter 38

Somehow the battered, old Morris Minor had made the 100-mile journey to Stoke. Jake had been squashed into the back seats with all their paraphernalia, whilst Phil and Dave enjoyed the relative comfort of the front. They had arrived just after midnight following an eventful journey during which the car's heating system decided to conk out and Jake was beginning to wonder if this was such a good idea.

Jake had seen Phil and Dave in the King's Head on several previous occasions but had never had reason to get to know them, as he was always there with his own mates. Times had changed for Jake. He had often thought that they looked like a couple of 'poofs'. They certainly dressed differently from him with their slightly longer hair and 'ladies' shoes: brown slip-ons, each with two tassels! Their only saving grace was that they fed the juke box and played the music which stirred Jake's inner electricity: soul. Jake left them alone, unlike other clientele of the King's Head who he didn't like the look of.

One Saturday night Jake sat alone at the bar nursing a pint of 'Tartan' when the two 'poofs' arrived just after

9.30 pm. A bit late to come out Jake thought, not much drinking time left.

'What'll it be boys?' asked Trevor, ever the genial 'Mein host' of the King's Head.

'Two cokes please,' replied Phil,' confirmed, thought Jake, Poofs! 'We're driving up to Stoke later.' Phil completed, either side of Jake's thought process.

'What's happening there?' enquired Trevor, in complete ignorance as to why anyone in their right mind would want to go to Stoke on a cold, wet Saturday at that time of night.

'An all-nighter at The Torch,' said Dave. Trevor looked none the wiser and carried on rubbing the inside of a pint mug with his dirty tea towel.

Jake's ears pricked up on two counts: Phil had just returned to the bar from the juke box in the corner and 'Smokey' was now soulfully lamenting 'The Tears of a Clown'. The news about an all-night drinking session was also music to his ears.

'Got room for a little one?' somewhat bravely enquired Jake, never one to push himself into a conversation unless he was in charge.

'For what?' asked Dave.

'The all-night drinking session,' was Jake's ignorant response. The two 'poofs' roared with laughter at Jake's misunderstanding.

'We're going to an all-night Northern Soul gig in Stoke', Phil eventually blurted out, once their laughter had died down.

'Well yeh,' said Jake turning slightly red, 'I knew that, but there will be drink?' he asked hopefully.

'There'll be drink for sure, but we go for the music and to dance,' said Phil. Definite 'poofs' then, thought Jake.

'We do have a spare seat if you're really interested?' said Phil, 'But you'll have to chip in with some petrol money.' He added.

'How much? asked Jake, feeling in his pocket and knowing he had only about £3 left after being paid yesterday. He could always borrow some from his 'bank' in the morning for the rest of the week.

'A pound should cover it,' replied Phil, who would be driving his mother's car. He would inform her later.

'Ok I'm in,' Jake declared, as if their going was conditional on his declaration.

'We're leaving as soon as we finish these drinks at about 10,' Phil instructed, 'and have a piss before we set off because we aren't stopping until we get there.' He further instructed. There was more to these two than Jake had originally assumed from their appearance.

'Smokey' had long since finished 'wiping his tears' as the three were through the pub door, in the car and away down the A123.

The Morris pulled to halt on a piece of waste land behind a dilapidated wooden fence, beyond which stood a council estate and more specifically a parade of shops.

'Is this it?' Jake asked, desperate to stretch his constricted legs.

'Keep quiet, and stay there,' Phil said. He was very good at instruction thought Jake.

The two of them calmly got out of the car and in a practised move were over the fence before Jake could see through the gloomy night what they were up to. He thought he heard the sound of breaking glass, but that could have come from anywhere. They were probably having a piss.

Ten minutes later they were back in the car. Jake had heard a dog bark as they clambered the fence and ran to the safety of the car. They were breathing heavily and seemed excited. Perhaps they'd had a 'quickie', thought Jake still not convinced his previous view of them was not the correct one.

'That'll be 50p and hide these on you somewhere,' this time Dave was the one giving out the instruction. He handed Jake a handful of small blue tablets.

'But I haven't got a headache,' innocently said Jake. Phil and Dave looked at each other and creased with more laughter.

'Well you will have later, and you'll thank me for those.' Dave said in a more serious tone. Jake knew when to shut up with these two. He paid up and hid the pills.

They sat in the car for a few minutes waiting and listening. Nothing else moved. So, they did. Slowly they drove away from the gloom and re-entered the world of street lights.

Jake noticed they passed a sign declaring 'Tunstall'. They continued toward the high street and Phil stopped the car at a hotel car park.

'Are we here now?' asked Jake, hesitantly.

Phil and Dave got out of their respective seats and Dave pulled his seat forward to free Jake from his recent incarceration. He needed that piss now. The two removed their belongings which had accompanied Jake on the back seat. Jake had nothing with him. They each carried a cardboard box containing sleeved records. Jake had sneaked a look and seen the singles, all with large holes where a smaller one should have been. How can you play these he thought? They also each carried a handled, zipped bag adorned with various badges some of which displayed a clenched black, fist. Jake was puzzled and intrigued. He felt naked with nothing to carry.

'Can I help?' he asked the two of them.

'Fuck off!' was the immediate, simultaneous response as they each clutched their respective baggage with a stronger attachment.

They left the hotel and turned right into Hose Street, and there it was in all its splendour: 'The Golden Torch'. The sign was emblazoned on the front of a 1960's building having all the charm of a worn-out bingo hall.

'What a dump,' he said as they approached the glass panelled doors. Phil and Dave had felt the same on their first visit to 'heaven' and merely grinned at each other.

'There aren't many people about,' observed Jake.

'Not at this time,' replied Phil, 'it's been open a few hours and that's why we get here later, to avoid the queues,' he lied.

They pushed open the front doors with all the

confidence of regulars, Jake took up the rear. A muffled beat hit Jake's ears immediately as he entered the building. They were confronted with a trestle table behind which sat two grumpy looking grandparents, or so Jake thought. They had to be called George and Mildred! George wore a school teacher's check jacket complete with leather elbow patches, a check shirt and a Windsor- knotted tie. He had grey hair and wore steel rimmed glasses. Mildred was of the blue rinse brigade, wearing a flowery pinafore skirt. She peered at the three new entrants over the top of her glasses and declared:

'That's 35 pence each please,' they handed her the money which she quickly deposited into an overflowing bucket under the table. George tore off raffle tickets as receipt and handed them out in order.

Phil and Dave casually entered the main hall through the double doors, thus leaving Jake to make his virgin entrance alone.

He walked through and immediately stopped just inside the door. His mouth gaped open as he took it all in, through every one of his senses. His eyes, nose and ears went everywhere:

A massive sea of people in a gyrating, musical bubble. He couldn't move from the spot as he absorbed the smell: a concoction of sweat, smoke and atmosphere. The latter was as tangible as the first two. He felt a drip on his head and looked up at the brown, stained stalactites of nicotine and water leaking down. There was white powder everywhere on the bouncing dance floor which was completely filled with bodies, but somehow seemed individually spaced, in a massive throng of movement the like of which he had never witnessed before. He thought he was good, but these 'guys and dolls' were, to put it mildly, unbelievable.

It was the 'guys' who struck him first. They were spinning, bouncing, treading across air, falling and springing back up, they were diving forward and in one move were back upright. His eyes couldn't keep up with the speed of their feet. He'd seen similar moves on 'Top of the Pops' by the likes of Jackie Wilson, The Temptations and others singing the songs he loved; but these were ordinary guys from places like him and they were better than the telly ones. They seemed more passionate and completely free. He knew that feeling.

Then it hit him, the sound. The four-beat came to his ears and he rocked. 'What is that? he thought, as his whole body tuned into it. Everybody in that throng of revolving people was in tune to the rhythm and clapped in wondrous unison as 'Gloria' declared something about a 'love being tainted'. Jake instinctively joined them, and her, with that handclap in a display of mutual, orgasmic outpouring. Jake was hooked and elated.

He turned to watch as Phil and Dave effortlessly blended with the multitude on the dance floor. Whilst Jake had merely stood in amazement, they had deposited their baggage and changed into their kit: They wore their coloured vests. 'Poofs' crossed his mind again. And, 'What were those trousers all about?' he thought: Baggy and swirling as they moved, worn high at the waist. In their tasselled shoes they glided effortlessly across the floor in complete harmony with the sound. They were gone and he so wanted to join them.

He suddenly felt isolated in his cumbersome boots and overbearing Crombie, in the incredible heat of the hall. He needed a drink to help take it all in.

He found the bar at the back of the hall where another member of the 'George and Mildred' clan was in attendance.

'Pint of 'Tartan,' please.' He innocently asked.

'What, you having a laugh?' replied granddad. 'Coca Cola or lemonade is all you'll get here son'. Jake was sure they had said there would be drink.

'I'll have a pint of coke then.' The first eye opener for Jake. He downed it in one as he usually did with his first pint of 'Tartan'. Feeling, only slightly, refreshed he continued taking in what was happening around him. 'How can I ever be part of this?' he pondered, as he watched the 'dolls' in their long flowing dresses and ankle socks match the guys with every beat. He even glimpsed a pair of white knickers, as a lone dancer pirouetted to the fantastic sound ringing around. Another bonus of coming here, he said to himself.

He must have stood watching, dumbstruck, for a couple of hours when his bladder called out to him. He found the toilet and entered. A tall, slim man and a rather chunkier side-kick, greeted him as he entered.

'Not seen you before,' slim man said. 'Who the fuck are you?' he added sneeringly. Jake usually asked questions in that manner and for once felt well out of his comfort zone.

'I just came in here for a piss,' he replied.

'Nobody just comes in here for a piss,' retorted Slim Man, as Sidekick moved menacingly toward Jake simultaneously feeling in his pocket.

'Buy or fuck off,' were the choices offered by Slim Man. Jake was not one for being intimidated but a change had come over him the second he came through those double doors of the hall. He wanted more of this feeling and for once felt discretion definitely seemed the best form of valour. Although he didn't have a clue what they were suggesting he 'buy', the second option seemed the most appropriate. He exited the toilet and went back to the womb-like cacophony of sound, heat and movement. He so wanted to strut onto that floor and disappear into the music like he had so many times before to the songs he knew. He thought he knew every new single and hit, after all he listened to the 'Top Thirty' show every Sunday evening on Radio One and taped them on his Ferguson recorder. These songs were all alien to him, but they filtered into his very soul and his whole being responded. He would not stop now.

He was beginning to feel the strain of the night and sensed a bit of a headache coming on. He remembered the tablets he'd popped into his pocket and decided to pop a couple into his mouth. That should do the trick he thought.

Phil and Dave were nowhere to be seen in the mass of bodies on the dance floor. He'd find them later. Jake looked up at the large clock, high above the stage at the front of the hall. It showed 4 o'clock but he couldn't quite work out if that was morning or afternoon. His headache had cleared, and he felt good but confused.

He continued his 'magical mystery tour' around the various rooms of the hall, avoiding the toilet where he had encountered the local Mafia. He had found an alternative outlet for his bladder contents outside the hall near to an oak tree, which had obviously had several previous visitors judging by the smell!

Back inside the building Jake came across another room which was packed with a sweating, multitude of bodies together with the accompanying buzz of conversation. There were tables everywhere and each seemed stacked with brown cardboard boxes filled with ordered rows of sleeves holding the 'jewels'. He watched in silent awe as the buying, selling, bartering and exchanging took place. In some cases, he witnessed small packets of pills being exchanged for a 'jewel'. This was the 'sale' room and the 'jewel' was the much sought after 7-inch piece of plastic which produced those sounds still pumping out in the other room. The single record, two and a half minutes of aural pleasure to those who knew and appreciated. There was genuine love in that room for the products on sale and Jake was desperate to understand. He joined the browsers looking at the unknown, to him, names, songs and labels of those precious commodities. Time just vanished in that room as he tried to appear knowledgeable for once. He bought nothing. His heady feeling returned but a couple more of his tablets soon sorted that.

He returned to the main hall where the throng was still lost in its world and as the DJ announced something about '3 for 8'. He wasn't sure if he'd heard right but it was then coming up to ten to eight and perhaps the DJ was simply giving a time check?

The floor immediately became completely saturated with moving bodies. Jake being forced to the edge of the dance area to simply watch alone, as the dancers entered their trance like worlds and 'disappeared'. He'd already spotted his two 'mates' on the floor, well he'd be coming again with them and felt comfortable to list them as such.

'Definitely not 'poofs,' he thought.

He couldn't believe that he'd been there for nearly eight hours and still felt so high. The chorus of the penultimate song declared 'Time will pass you by' and, to Jake, it seemed so appropriate. The final rendition of the night left everybody feeling exhausted and refreshed at the same time.

The lights went on at 8 am on the dot. The hall was awash with people stripping off, towelling themselves down, and shaking talcum powder over their sweaty bodies. Their 'street' clothes were retrieved from those handled, zipped bags and replaced with their soiled dance togs.

'Ready,' said Phil to Jake who stood gawping at the end of the night as he had at the start. Dave came over still wiping his mop of sweat drenched hair, before shoving the towel back into his bag.

'Yep,' was all Jake could muster after an experience he could never put into words. A feeling of wanting to belong is all he could come up with.

'Let's get going then,' said Phil. As the Morris sped off down the road, with Jake once again taking the back seat with all the luggage. He didn't mind at all. On the return journey he was much more appreciative of his position in this group!

'How's the headache?' enquired Dave. They both laughed in unison.

Chapter 39 ~ 1974

Life was certainly a bit different for Mary nowadays. The shop and working with mum remained unchanged, although Rory was continuing to become more of a presence. He had even started to come into the shop occasionally to 'give us girls' a hand, as mum put it. Mary simply smiled and quite often left them to it. She was happy for her mum.

Mary had heard via Jake that both Drip and Fergie had gone off to join the army. She had, by now, come to terms with the 'incident' with Drip, and following his departure had decided to try to forget it happened. She still, foolishly, felt part-responsible for tempting him. She certainly wouldn't miss either of them. Mary also knew that Jake would be even lonelier now that his only real mates had moved on with their lives.

She had always known that Will would have far more work to do as he approached the end of his course and would get home less often. It was still, however, very hard to go for such long periods of time without seeing him. He phoned, occasionally, of course and told her about his life at university; with always at least one mention of Erica. She was a mystery to Mary. Who was she? What did she mean to Will? Was she a threat? Was Will slowly, but surely, working to dump her and continue his dream with another free spirit? These and many thoughts haunted Mary, who sensed the cell door creaking again.

She had actually started to look forward to her Wednesday 'date' night with Jake. He was always so punctual, and the evenings continued along the same pattern as all the others. They would take the bus into town and quickly deposit the takings at Lloyds, before finding a different pub each week to enjoy a drink together. Mary was beginning to feel that these were like proper dates, especially now that Jake seemed so much less aggressive than he used to. She often wondered if the new, slightly longer hair style and the tasselled tan loafers, not to mention the smarter trousers and sweaters, were down to her influence.

The 'Northern Soul' certainly wasn't.

Since Jake had 'discovered' this 'way of life', it seemed it was all he wanted to talk about.

Not like the 'old' Jake who would stay silent for what seemed like hours. At least he seemed enthused about something on their dates, and after a while Mary felt tempted to go with him to an 'all-nighter'. He, for some reason, convinced her that this wasn't a good idea given she needed to be up so early for the morning papers and these gigs went on all night, you know!

'As if the name wasn't a giveaway,' she thought.

Nevertheless, Mary found herself interested to listen to him talk endlessly about the soul music, the dance moves, especially by the lads and the record sale room.

Jake even brought along his 'Adidas' bag and showed his 'bags', his vest and even his talcum powder!

'What's that for?' she asked.

'Stops me stinking after a long session,' he replied.

'There was no answer to that,' thought Mary.

'Does that mean they play Diana Ross and Stevie Wonder records all night?' she innocently asked him one night.

His face spoke a thousand words in reply and his look said, 'she would never get it'. She didn't!

'Is there Southern Soul too?' she ventured, in an attempt to really wind him up. He didn't bite, he merely nudged his head upwards raising his eyes at the same time.

Mary liked music, she didn't love music. She had the same indifference to Will when he harped on about some rock band he'd seen the previous week at the union bar. Mary liked what she liked and wouldn't pigeon hole any of it. Will and Jake were at last in agreement, they couldn't understand that she didn't share their respective musical passions.

So, with the 'new' Jake in tow she began to really enjoy the times out with him and after several trips to the town the drink became two and eventually, they would finish the night with a burger or a bag of chips before bussing home. Mary had even begun to give Jake a peck on the cheek after he had escorted her home. There was, however, something very different about Jake: It wasn't just his endless conversation about the weekly jaunts up North with 'Phil and Dave', even that sounded like a soul band she thought, or even his new-found dress sense. It wasn't just the fact that he never seemed to have any money to pay his share on their nights out, as he used to. After all, he was accompanying her to the bank as a favour and so she was quite happy to pay for the evening. It was something in his eyes, which always looked so far away and sometimes he would actually fall asleep on the bus on the way home. She enjoyed their time together but............

On one very wet, Wednesday evening just as Mary was finishing up for the night, the bell on the inside of the shop's door rang to indicate the presence of a customer. Mary looked up and there stood Jake.

'I was a bit early and didn't fancy waiting at the bus stop in this rain, so thought I'd pop in and surprise you,' he offered by means of explanation seeing the puzzled look on Mary's face.

'That's ok,' replied Mary 'I've nearly finished,' she said opening the till and placing some notes in it, in readiness for tomorrow morning.

'I'll just have to pop upstairs and tell Mum we're off,' she added.

As soon as she was through the door leading to the upstairs flat Jake took his chance and went to the till, he grabbed a couple of fivers and stuffed them into the pocket of his black 'Sta-Prest'. He pushed the till shut and returned to his original position on the other side of the counter. He stood nonchalantly staring at a row of magazines on the rack, with both hands casually placed in his trouser pockets, as Mary came back down.

She smiled as she walked toward him.

'After you,' he said, politely ushering her through the door. She closed the door behind her as Jake put up the umbrella. Mary fed her hand through his bent arm, tilted her head towards his muscled arm and together they headed to the bus stop.

'I'm sure I left that till open,' she thought to herself as she sat on the bus, simultaneously moving her thigh slightly away from Jake's. She suddenly felt uneasy.

Jake gave himself an inward grin and patted his pocket.

Chapter 40

He never felt a thing. He had been the meat in the sectarian sandwich.

The bullet entered his skull between the eyes and exited via his brain producing a gaping hole and an expulsion of his head's contents onto the brick wall behind him, where moments before he had stood. His lifeless body slumped to the ground. A final dribble of snot fell from his nose and landed on the badge of his green beret, which had been scraped from his head as it was dragged down the brick wall.

Drip had taken to army life like a duck to water. He had had to get away from his previous, unfulfilled life going nowhere and under the control of Jake. Of course, at the time, he had been saved from a life of being bullied and inconsequentiality by attaching himself to Jake and Fergie, but that eventually only led to more frustration of his lot. He also needed to forget. The army had given him a purpose, he felt needed. It was easy: you did what you were told, and life was good. He'd become an independent man who could stand by himself and make disciplined judgements. He didn't need the crutch or protection of Jake. His new-found comrades took him for what he was, not what they could control. He was known as 'Jonno' now. John George Black it read on his birth certificate, not 'Drip' as Jake had christened him so many years before.

He'd surprised himself by sailing through his 'Basic Training' stint and was destined for the 'Light Infantry' on completion of 'Phase two'. Twenty-six weeks since waving goodbye to Jake he was prepared to go where the army sent him with his fellow soldiers. He was something, he was a soldier and he was also an enemy.

Sunday 30th January 1972 had changed everything in Northern Ireland. Both sides of the religious divide now had a legitimate target: The British Army, hitherto deployed to keep the peace. 'Bloody Sunday' christened them with all the blame of that momentous day. "The truth is a halfway house between them and us".

'Jonno' was only a soldier and like everyone else he'd seen the constant news footage on TV of 'The Troubles' and like many others tended to forget it once the TV was off. He did what he was told and bided his time with his many duties.

Tensions in Northern Ireland had risen dramatically ever since 'that day' in Derry. More and more troops needed to be deployed in an attempt to stem the growing violence. It was like a horrific, nightmarish football match of extreme hate played out on the streets: Catholics v Protestants, United Ireland v United Kingdom, IRA v UVF, Everyone v The Army. A battle for territory played out for the world to watch on TV, with the Army as the embattled referee and with ordinary people trying to work, rest and play around it all.

When the eventual call to arms came for 'The Light Infantry' to be deployed, they did what all good soldiers do, exactly as they were told.

After being flown out from Brize Norton the unit duly arrived after a very short flight. It somehow seemed further away on TV! The 'accommodation' was adequate, and they awaited instruction:

The four members of 'Jonno's' brick were driven to the area between the roads of Falls and Shankhill in West Belfast. They carried their protection with the love and attention weeks of training had imbedded.

'Jonno' caressed his 'SLR 7.62mm' as he followed his three comrades, criss-crossing over the road to avoid any 'cross hairs' settling on his body. They moved in silence, eyes darting like a rabbit's in a field of danger. On signal they each crouched by a protective wall to observe, listen and watch.

He never saw the sniper high above in the derelict factory opposite from where he was positioned. He had temporarily stood to relieve cramp in his left calf, as he stood to stretch the muscle the unseen cross hairs fixed on his brow and the anonymous AR-18 fired.

'Jonno' took the short, return flight home in a box. It was covered with a Union Jack when he was driven across the tarmac.

He was 20 years old and had paid for his past mistakes.

Chapter 41

'A soldier has been killed in Northern Ireland,' announced the eloquent BBC newsreader from the radio, as Mary counted out the 'Daily Mirrors' into the sacks for the morning paper round boys.

'John George Black was shot and killed whilst on duty in the Shankhill Road area of West Belfast, he was twenty years old and from Northwich, England. He served in the Light Infantry and was on his first tour of duty. It is believed he was shot by sniper fire.'

'Younger than me and from around here, I wonder whose son he was?' thought Mary as she moved on to count out the 'Daily Mails'.

'His body will be flown home and buried in his home town with a private service,' continued the radio announcer.

'And now for the weather in your area,' he concluded.

Mary had been first one down next morning. Her mum was still 'faffing' around with her hair, no doubt for Rory's sake! Mary had doubled checked the notes and they appeared to be ten pounds short. She checked again.

She tried to convince herself that perhaps, in her hurry to leave, she had made a mistake. She decided to leave it until next week.

The following Wednesday duly arrived, and Jake was as punctual as ever. He seemed to always come into the shop now irrespective of the weather.

'Hi Jake,' said Mary as he appeared through the door, 'Won't be a minute, just get my coat and the bag from the back,' she added.

As soon as Mary went through the door to the flat, Jake was over the counter. He knew exactly how to open the till. Three five-pound notes went straight into his pocket. The 'headache' pills were costing him more and more.

Mary had deliberately left the door to the flat very slightly ajar allowing her to peer through and observe Jake in action. As he stuffed the notes into his trouser pocket, she pushed the door open and stood six inches from him.

'What are you doing?' she asked as he stood, both hands in his pockets, on her side of the counter.

'Er, I wanted a closer look at the sweets,' he sheepishly replied. 'What's in your pocket?' knowingly she enquired.

'Nothing,' was the reply she anticipated. 'Let me see then,' she said.

'Fuck you, you fucking bitch,' he screamed, 'You're like the fucking rest of them!'

As he screamed the words at her, he removed a tightly clenched fist from his right-hand pocket and threw the three crumpled notes into Mary's face. His eyes showed that evil look she had not seen for a long time. She was very scared in that moment.

He formed a fist again and drew his arm back lifting it towards her face. Mary instinctively flinched away. Jake saw his own Mother's face in that moment.

'Fuck you,' he repeated. He relaxed his fist, dropped his tense arm, leapt over the counter and out of the door. The bell, at the top of the door, nearly came off its perch as he slammed it shut with an angry, forceful yank.

Carol immediately came hurtling down the stairs to find out what the commotion was all about. The bell had just stopped its ring as she opened the door into the shop to find Mary crumpled behind it. She lifted Mary to her feet and held her tightly.

Mary calmed down and explained the whole saga. Carol gave no opinion, she just supported her daughter.

'He didn't touch me Mum,' almost defending Jake's actions. 'Well I'll come with you tonight to the bank,' Carol said.

'We'll shut up shop and have a girl's night out,' she continued.

Jake seemed to have disappeared from the face of the earth as far as Mary was concerned. He never appeared for his usual morning paper and certainly there was no sign of him on the following Wednesday.

Mary told Carol that she would carry on with the banking as usual and set off with the takings under her cardigan in the shopping basket to catch the bus. Carol had been concerned but Mary insisted that Jake would not change her life one iota. She was still convinced that he would never hurt her.

As she waited alone at the bus-stop she didn't notice him creep up beside where she stood. ' What's in the basket?' he asked calmly, almost knowingly.

Somewhat startled Mary looked up at where the voice had come from. She saw a pair of recognisable, evil eyes from under a peaked hat but on an older face.

'I said what's in the fucking bag?' the intruder demanded more menacingly. 'Nothing except my cardigan,' Mary offered. 'I'm going shopping,' she added.

'Give us the fucking bag and I'll have a look myself,' he said trying to grab the basket. Mary clung onto it with all her life.

'Gimme the fucking thing,' he demanded again. She wouldn't relinquish hold.

She saw him clench his fist and he drew his arm back lifting it towards her face. As it moved towards her face a muscled arm came from nowhere and grabbed it away from her. The hand unclenched as its owner's arm was twisted into a painful position and he was thrown to the ground.

'Who the fuck are you?' he said getting to his feet and diving towards the new 'intruder', with his hand clenched again, ready for attack. Before he could even raise his arm the 'intruder's' fist caught him first, smack on the nose and he quickly returned to ground.

'The lady doesn't want to share her bag, now I suggest you get up and get out of here before we call the police,' said the 'Knight in shining armour'.

'Oh, and to answer your polite question, I am Corporal Derek Ferguson of 2 Para.' 'Now run,' he completed his final advice for the night.

Mary stood in shock at what had happened and the thought of what might have happened without Corporal Derek Ferguson arriving on the scene when he did.

'It could only have been Jake who told him,' she said to herself, as Joe Kirke ran for his life down the street.

'Fergie, is that you?' asked Mary when she had recovered. She could see it now as he stood under the full glare of the street light. The same shaped face and that very serious look. Of course, he looked bigger and stronger. The uniform gave him that air of confidence and she suddenly felt as safe and secure with him as she had done more recently with Jake.

'Jake had forsaken the one thing that bonds two people as much as love. He had now lost her trust for ever,' she thought.

'The self-same Fergie,' he offered, 'and still known as Fergie to this day.'

She looked up to him with total admiration and gratitude. He had come a long way since he was number two to Jake when they ruled the estate. He looked so handsome now in that deliberately tilted red beret with its winged parachute emblem.

'What are you doing here?' she asked.

'Compassionate leave, to visit Jonno's parents,' he answered. 'I'm sure you heard what happened to him in Northern Ireland.'

'Who's Jonno?' she asked somewhat puzzled.

'Oh sorry, you probably remember him as Drip,' he replied.

'The twenty-year-old from Northwich,' she remembered from the radio, as the penny finally dropped.

'Yes, I heard it on the news, very sad,' she said with mixed emotions as she also remembered the park on that awful night.

' Drip and Jonno were obviously completely different people,' she told herself thinking of his devastated parents and, as usual, not herself.

'I was trying to find Jake to ask him if he wanted to come with me, as we were all close once upon a time. I can't find him anywhere and was on my way to the shop to ask when I spotted you at the bus stop,' he explained.

'Haven't seen him for a while,' Mary lied.

'What was his dad up to, bothering you like that?' He felt almost obliged to ask her, given what had just happened.

Once again Mary felt compelled to fully explain, as the 18.16 went sailing past at 18.27 without stopping.

'We should have definitely called the police then,' said Fergie when Mary had finished relating the whole story for the second time that day.

'I'll call in at the station tomorrow, meanwhile I insist on going with you to the bank,' said Fergie.

'Okay,' said Mary. She was grateful for his company but knew who she needed more than anyone at that moment.

Chapter 42

Will had always thought Gaynor was odd, or did he really mean different? He should have learnt from his previous experience and never to judge until he knew all her facts! He was still convinced, however, that she was different, but he couldn't put his finger on exactly what made her different. She could be in his company but somehow seemed 'gone'. 'Then again,' he thought, Erica had that same mystifying quality.

Gaynor was a couple of years older than both Will and Erica. She had already completed her degree in 'Social Studies' before they had even arrived at Durham. She was now working toward her PhD, investigating: 'The effects of social, political and economic influences on undergraduate lifestyles and the subsequent repercussions for democracy'. She had inside information on that one!

Gaynor Ansell-Collins heralded from a very privileged background. She had attended Wycombe Abbey Public School for girls (only) and graduated with four grade A's at A-level. She had subsequently, and rather arrogantly, turned down a place at Corpus Christi College, Oxford. This was much to the disgust of her parents, the recently separated Henry and Sybil Ansell-Collins. Gaynor cited that she needed to 'mix with other types' as the reason for this decision. Durham had been just about acceptable to her parents. They duly packed their 'princess' off and into her luxury flat in the centre of the city, within easy walking distance of the university. The flat had been bought by Henry. Sybil would additionally provide Gaynor with an adequate allowance. No state grant needed for her. Gaynor had lived on her own for a couple of years but even she got lonely and decided to rent the two spare bedrooms. Erica and Malcolm were perfect applicants and after a quick interview everybody was happy with the arrangement. She took Erica under her wings! She tolerated the presence of Drake.

Will ambled into the Union bar one Tuesday night as arranged. He picked up his pint and casually walked across to their usual table where he would find Erica. There she was and as visually delightful as always. There was an extra buzz in the bar tonight and certainly far more people than previous Tuesdays.

'It must be getting near the end of the year,' he thought as he continued his walk toward the table, where he noticed that someone else was sitting next to Erica. 'Are they holding hands?' he asked himself as he approached.

'Oh, it's just Gaynor,' he thought. He actually liked Gaynor, in a strange way, and she had warmed to him too, eventually. He never seemed intimidated by her background and actually stood up to her. In return she respected him, but he always sensed the protective barrier she erected around Erica.

The two girls were giggling loudly when he finally rested his glass of lager and lime on the beer mat in front of him. He noticed an empty bottle of 'Blue Nun' on the table and a second bottle was already being emptied.

Two other glasses were set aside, and he smelled the characteristic aniseed odour in the air.

'Having a good night, ladies?' he asked, taking a tentative sip of his drink. The girls giggled in response, before Gaynor responded:

'We're celebrating the end of the year Will, have a glass of vino!' 'No thanks,' he replied. 'I'll stick to my lager,' he added.

'…and lime!' the two girls mockingly said in unison, accompanied by more giggles.

It was then that Will noticed the folded newspaper on the table being carefully guarded by Gaynor. He didn't attempt to take it to read this time.

Erica and Gaynor were in their own little world as the second bottle of wine disappeared down their respective throats. Will sipped his beer. He noticed that the bar was really filling up as a band began setting up on the stage behind them. He sat in silence, pleased to be around Erica but feeling slightly uncomfortable until he felt a pat on the shoulder and a recognisable voice declared:

'Will, my old man, how the Dickens are you this fine evening!'

Miguel and the Prof had finally finished all of their academic work and were out on a 'school night'.

'Thank God for that,' thought Will, rescued at last. The boys sat down, uninvited, at the table.

'Hi ladies,' said Miguel

They both giggled in reply and took another slurp of wine. The Prof attempted to pick up the paper, but the look, not to mention the stamp of Gaynor's hand on it, made him leave it exactly where it was.

'We're going to 'Annabelle's' in town, are you coming Will,' were the first comprehensible words spoken by Erica so far since he had sat down.

Will was tempted to go with Erica, but he sensed he wasn't really being asked.

'I'll stay with the boys and check the band out,' he said, 'haven't seen them before and it'll be good to have a boys' night before we all go home for the summer.'

Gaynor smiled, she picked up the folded paper and put her other hand out towards Erica. She held the hand as Erica leant forward to give Will a peck on his cheek. She walked into the chair as they moved away, and they were definitely holding hands as they moved across the dance floor.

'Right, let's get this party on the road,' declared Miguel returning from the bar with a tray of drinks. The band struck up the opening riff.

The boys danced and drank, they laughed and cried with more laughter. All those days together finally coming to a conclusion, just like their respective dissertations, which were all now distant memories. They were ready for the real world.

'I've had enough,' said Will at 2.30 am. 'I'm going back to the flat.'

'I'll join you,' said an equally knackered Prof. Miguel was playing 'tongue fencing' with one of the first-year students. He'd long since forgotten he was meant to meet Janice at the Odeon to see 'The Towering Inferno' at 8 o'clock!

It was 11.30 am when the shrill of the phone woke everyone except Miguel. The Prof answered it as Will came yawning through from his room at the same time as an unknown female emerged from Miguel's room. Will noticed she was wearing Miguel's rugby shirt. Miguel merely snored loudly and rolled over.

'It's for you, Will. I think it's Gaynor,' said the Prof passing the green phone over to Will. 'Hello, what's up,' he asked between yawns and scratching his groin under his Y fronts. 'Oh my God, I'm coming straight over,' he screamed into the phone mouthpiece. 'What's happened?' asked a startled Prof, 'can I do anything?' he felt he had to ask.

'No, I have to get over there,' said Will pulling on a pair of someone's jeans he had found on the floor and borrowing the girl's rugby shirt. He noticed she was wearing nothing underneath.

He took the bike he found propped up outside the backdoor and peddled as fast as he could to Gaynor's flat. He had no idea what colour the traffic lights were, but he didn't stop anywhere.

There was an ambulance parked outside the block of flats and the security locked front door was wedged open. He ran up the stairs to the flat.

The ambulance men were just leaving, they both shook their heads as they passed Will in the corridor. A police constable stood at the door guarding the entrance to the flat.

'You can't go in young man, I'm sorry, we have to wait for the forensic team to check things before we can move her,' politely said PC 342.

Will stood helpless at the entrance to the flat peering down its long corridor, looking a bit strange in the oversized Levi's and the ridiculously undersized shirt. As usual he didn't care about his appearance.

His view of the toilet at the end of the flat was blocked by the presence of a female police officer whose outstretched arm cradled a shuddering and sobbing Gaynor.

Gaynor heard the voice of the police constable speaking to someone at the door and she turned to face him. She saw Will, broke away from the comforting hold of the police woman and ran to Will. They stood and embraced in each other's arms. They broke momentarily and stared at the 'Gypsy Queen'.

She was still seated proudly on her throne. Her white, silk knickers were still in position around her parted ankles. Her trademark long flowing dress made sure her modesty was well covered. Her arms were splayed out to her sides as she remained slumped against the china cistern behind. Her head was angled back against the wall. Her long black wavy hair straddled the cistern and was smeared with the same yellow bile and vomit which was encrusted in and around her beautiful lips. A trail of vomit had spread from the corner of her mouth onto her dimpled chin. Someone had kindly moved the hair from her face and closed her eye lids. Will would never see those beautiful eyes again.

As he looked at Erica for the final time, the coroner's report was concluded in his head:

'Cause of death: by inhalation of vomit.'

He broke away from Gaynor, kissed her on the cheek and left that devastating scene to find his own solace.

He knew who he needed more than anyone else at that moment.

Chapter 43

The District Coroner duly signed the report of Erica Patricia Madden:

'Cause of death: inhalation of her own vomit during a period of unconsciousness which led to pulmonary edema'. Will was almost right.

The body could now be released.

The funeral was arranged for the following week and would be held at the local church of Saint Mary's in Staindrop, County Durham. Erica had spent the first eighteen years of her life growing up in that village. She died eighteen miles from where she was born.

It was Will who rang first. Mary was in the shop and desperate for a break from work so she could find time to ring Will and make those arrangements to visit. It was almost two years since she had said she would go!

She needed him now, she had to get away from the shadow of Jake and she needed Will to hold her and tell her it would be all right.

'Hello, it's me,' said Will before she could even speak.

'Something terrible has happened and I need you

with me,' he continued.

'I need to be with you too Will, I've had problems with Jake, and I have to get away for a while,' she said.

'Can you come at the weekend and stay for the funeral, I really want you to be with me on that day?' he pleaded. 'It's being held up here on Sunday, please say yes,' he rambled.

'Slow down, Will, whose funeral?'

'Erica, my friend has died,' he replied.

'Her!' thought Mary.

'That's terrible, of course I'll come but how did it happen?'

'Can we talk when you are here, and what's he been up to now?'

'We'll talk when we meet Will,' said Mary, 'That'll be best for both of us.'

'I'll get the train up and you can meet me at the station, okay?' she continued.

'Just let me know when and I'll be there,' said Will, 'I love you Mary Rodgers,' he added. 'I love you too William Brown,' she replied.

They hung up simultaneously.

Mary cradled the receiver for a few minutes and immediately felt better for sharing with Will.

Will cradled the receiver for a few minutes and immediately felt better for sharing with Mary.

The 14.13 into Durham arrived, miraculously, on

time and there he was waiting. Mary spied Will before his eyes found her.

'Has he had a haircut?' she asked herself. Then he saw her, and his face beamed.

She was the first off the train and Will was waiting at the door. They didn't care that Mary's case had blocked the exit or that there was a queue to get off the train as they embraced until they were politely interrupted by,

'Er, excuse me could we all get off?' said a suited office worker desperate to get back to his desk.

Will grabbed her case and her hand and they got out of the way of the door, still oblivious to everyone else.

'We can walk to the flat,' declared Will, 'It's not far,' he added. 'Not for a cash-strapped student,' he didn't add!

The 'short' walk along the river and through the beautiful city towards Will's flat, gave them both the opportunity to tell their respective tales. Will heard all about the situation with Jake and Mary listened, with mixed emotions, about the tragic death of Erica. Their hands tightened as they listened to each other's story.

The flat was empty when they arrived as both boys had, conveniently, gone home for the weekend.

Will dropped the case as they entered and turned to face Mary. She removed her coat and moved toward him. Their lips met and time stood still. All their built-up emotion and passion of the last three years of living different lives, exploded into the wonderful climax of uninhibited making of love. They laid entwined for what seemed an eternity afterwards.

191

Mary woke first and slowly lifted the sheets from the single bed, trying not to disturb the still sleeping Will. She stood and looked around his life, distilled into the contents of this tiny room. The first thing to strike her was the number of books on the numerous shelves all around the walls: Coleoptra, Lepidoptra, Diptera, British, Northern European, every possible combination of the insect family covered somewhere on those shelves. Mary moved across to Will's desk and there it was, another book she hadn't seen for years and 'he still had it on display,' she thought.

A tatty, paper covered reading book took pride of place on the desk:

'Janet and John' proudly declared the title of the book. Mary noticed the handwritten scrawl declaring the owner's name: 'William Brown' and underneath, in an obviously different childish writing, someone had added: 'loves Mary'. She smiled as her hand rubbed across that long forgotten, but so true, message. She didn't open the book.

Will stirred and sat up. He smiled at the image before him and thought he was having one of his dreams. Then reality returned and he realised his vision this time was happening. Mary was here and in that moment life was good. Then Erica crossed his mind.

'What time is it? He asked her when his brain had returned to its rightful place. 'Twenty past ten,' replied Mary.

'And what day?' he further enquired still confused by the sight of Mary in his room.

'Sunday,'

'The day of the funeral then,' said Will.

St. Mary's Church sits in an idyllic setting on the main road of Staindrop surrounded by the rolling countryside of County Durham beyond. Mary and Will had been directed to their reserved second row seats at the front of the church. The vicar was already there making small talk with the occupants of the front rows on either side of the aisle.

Seated on one side was a dour looking man. 'Presumably Erica's step- father,' thought Will. On the same side of the aisle, but as far from him as possible, sat a beautifully elegant lady, dressed in a flowing black dress with matching hat. She had long black, curly hair resting on her upright back.' It had to be Erica's mother,' again thought Will. Immediately beside her, almost on guard, was the ever dutiful and protective 'Drake', although today he would undoubtedly be Malcolm.

Immediately in front of Will and Mary, and all alone with her thoughts, sat the equally graceful Gaynor. She too was attired in black in the form of a long elegant 'Aquascutum' coat. She wore no hat but even at this time of year she wore black gloves. 'How Erica inspired grace,' thought Will.

The vicar stood upright and sandwiched his bible between his praying hands as the coffin appeared at the door. On his nodded signal the verger lifted the arm of the record player and found the correct position on the black vinyl long player. The music had been requested by Gaynor, she didn't want the usual funeral dirge for her Erica. As the needle struck the opening circle of the track a crackling sound was relayed through the single speaker in front of the vicar to the captive congregation.

The singer lamented:

' And by the way before you go, I'd like to say

I love you so

If it's goodbye maybe for good I will not cry

Maybe I should

And I love you so'

Gaynor sobbed loudly and uncontrollably as the soulful words of the song enveloped the church. She had nobody to comfort her. Mary caressed Will's hand as she spotted tears rolling down his cheeks.

After the emotional ceremony the coffin was taken to its final resting place and Erica was given back to the earth. The tears fell again as each person threw a handful of soil onto the coffin's top. Malcolm supported his mother as his father moved away from their lives.

Gaynor felt the ring on her finger and wiped her tears away again. She turned to Will, who was being protectively comforted by Mary. Gaynor walked towards them at the edge of the grave.

She kissed Will on both cheeks and turned to Mary.

'You must be Will's Mary? I've heard so much about you.' She kissed her on one cheek.

Gaynor turned back to Will and said, 'Erica loved you like her brother, but we were in love.' She gently twisted the ring on her finger again, looked down into the grave, smiled 'because it happened', and walked away.

Mary knew then. Will realised everything now about Erica. The 'Gypsy Queen' was dead.

Will did his usual at the rail station and as Mary sat on the stationary train waiting to leave, he walked backwards on the platform waving to her as though the train was moving away. He thought it was hilarious. Who knows what the man sitting next to Mary thought!

As the guard blew his whistle, Will stood at the window his two hands splayed with open palms on the glass as he mouthed,

'I love you, see you when I get back,'

Mary mouthed in return 'I will always love you!'

The train departed on time.

Chapter 44

It was a bright cool day in August, and Mary's watch showed one o'clock. She knew he'd be late and, deliberately, she always arrived half an hour after his pre-arranged time. So when Will phoned to meet at 12.30 she knew when she would get there.

Mary had approached the 'Ravine' with some trepidation as she had not returned there since their 'goodbye' meeting, three long years ago when Will went off to university. She sat down on the edge of the Ravine which, unlike everything else in her life at that time, was completely unchanged from that last visit.

Will, of course, was nowhere to be seen.

Mary simply enjoyed the peace and the cool air which blew her long hair over her face. She looked across the 'Ravine' towards the wood trying to observe as Will would do. She didn't see the squirrel busily running up the Oak tree or the rabbit scurrying along with its eyes constantly looking for danger. She couldn't remember the names of all the wild flowers growing down the slope where she sat, although he'd told her so many times. But she did take the opportunity to remember the past three years and wonder.

The first year hadn't really changed very much in her life because she was always busy in the shop and Will seemed to be around just as much. Although he'd gone off to Durham, he had come back home every holiday to work in his Dad's factory and his holidays seemed to last for weeks. They'd meet and talk as if nothing was any different. Jake was still, at that time, on the periphery of their lives. A constant to them both in different ways. Mary had always given Jake the benefit of doubt in most situations whilst Will had merely tolerated him over the years. Will's love for Mary was stronger than anything Jake could attempt to break.

That second year was where the seeds were sown in so many different ways and her mind temporarily glossed over them for now, as another gust of cool air once again moved the hair across her face. She flicked it away with sharp nudge of her neck. The 'moment' was what mattered now, not the past.

Mary's mind travelled on to the better things that were happening in her life at this time. Carol, her mum, and 'the smile' had just announced that they were formally 'an item'. Mary had secretly known for months and was delighted for both of them. Carol had been so reluctant to admit that she could feel love for another man after her beloved husband, and father to her girls, Roy. In truth, Mary and her sister Lizzie had little tangible recollection of their dad, apart from a faded black and white photo perched on the shelf behind the television set. He'd never met Lizzie. 'The smile' was the affectionate name given to the newspaper delivery man by Mary and her mum. He appeared early every morning at the shop and Carol was always first out to receive the papers. She would grin for at least the next hour after he'd gone.

It started with her offering him a cup of tea one morning, which quickly became a daily habit. It took several months though before Rory (the smile) eventually plucked up the courage to invite Carol out for a drink. She said she wouldn't go without Mary's approval. Mary, of course, had told her mum that dad would want her to have a life without him, but she also remembered adding, 'never lose affection for people and things that went before'. She couldn't recollect where that mature piece of wisdom came from. In that moment Carol hugged Mary much tighter, and for much longer, than she had ever before. Her 'little' girl was now a woman. So when the 'formal' announcement came, both Mary and Lizzie pretended it was a 'nice surprise'. The happy couple 'wouldn't rush things' but an engagement would be next and then who knows! Mary's thoughts moved pleasurably on to her 'little' sister Lizzie who was no longer 'little', but a woman in her own right and about to embark on a university adventure of her own. Unlike Mary, Lizzie was blessed with academic ability and with encouragement from both Carol and Mary she had taken every opportunity to learn. She sailed through the 11 plus and everything else put in front of her and was now ready for her Cambridge experience. Nobody was prouder of Lizzie's achievements than Mary. Lizzie in turn hoped that there were good things around the corner for her 'big' sister.

She heard him before he arrived. He touched her left shoulder and sat down on her right. He thought it was so funny. Mary looked him in the eyes and tilted her head a split second before his lips found hers. Time stood still and they both relished the moment. As they moved slightly apart, she looked at him and thought how wonderful he was. The hair was still long, blond and straggling over his shoulders. She'd thought it before, but he was indeed a beautiful man both inside and out and he certainly was today. He would never win in the fashion stakes but in his own mind, he was well ahead of that game!

'Wotcha mate', were Will's first words as he gazed into those wonderful eyes. She never changes, he thought to himself, as he brushed her windblown hair from her face.

'How are you?' he continued.

'I'm fine', she replied and sighed as she wallowed in the contentment which enveloped her every time Will appeared in her life.

'What have you been thinking about sitting here?' Will asked. 'You' she replied, which was partly true.

'All good then?' he responded in his usual manner.

Will jiggled along from where they sat and reached for her responsive hand and held it as he always did with fingers entwined. They sat in mutual silence taking in the view, each lost in their separate thoughts. They had always been comfortable with silence as long as there was some contact.

Will's mind drifted back, and he also could remember that last meeting here as he thought about his life since. The first year away had been easy as he settled into life away from home. He loved being independent and thrived on making his own decisions. He also loved those seemingly endless holidays at home, where mum spoiled him rotten and he could spend time with Mary and Sam.

His new-found soul mates at university had made sure he was never lonely there although many of their collective exploits were best erased from memory! He had found the workload challenging but with his dedication and hard work he had got through. His final result confirmed his thoughts. He had achieved a 'First' in Entomology and was now ready to live his dream, but who with? He'd recently heard that his best mate, from what seemed a previous life, Sam had managed the identical result and was going to travel the world with the love of his life, Tom. Will had never realised that Sam had different preferences to his own and just regarded him as a true friend, ever since their 'Black and White Minstrel' days. Will had always been somewhat naive in the ways of the world.

The one area of his life which caused him the greatest concern was Erica. She would always be around the edge of his mind, but time would heal many of those scars. He was ready to move on and simply needed to put his proposition to Mary. He hoped it would be easier to convince her now about his plans.

Will thought, with affection, about his granddad, who had passed away last year. This in turn had led Will's father to consider his own future and he had finally decided that it was the right time to hand over control of the business and retire to their second home in Spain with his beloved wife Mags. Will's brother, James, was now running the business on his own and would stay in the family home with his own wife of four years, Jane. James had never wanted to simply follow in his dad's footsteps, but the reality was, he enjoyed hard work and the rewards it could bring. His previous 'dreams' had been quashed by material reality. No such thoughts for Will. His twin sister, Susan, had achieved her own success at university gaining a 2:1 in English. She had also 'gained' a man and they were going on their own trip across Europe in John's VW. Will prayed that they'd make it in that thing!

Will's new laid plan was to spend some time with his parents in Spain before embarking on his own adventure around the world. His idea was to take Mary on that first stage and slowly get her used to the idea of travelling the rest of the world with him. He knew it would be hard to persuade her but try his best, he would. After all, what did she have to keep her here?

He squeezed her hand as he planned the question formulating in his mind.

Jake strutted down the street towards the 'Ravine'. He'd called at the shop in the hope of speaking to Mary but was told by Rory that she had gone out to meet Will. Rory worked in the shop on Saturdays and it was he who had taken the call from Will. Jake knew exactly where they would meet, and he was not pleased.

Jake's fashion appearance nowadays was less aggressive as he had ditched his military-like attire of the recent past for a more presentable image. His hair was now more 'suede' than 'skin' and indeed was beginning to approach curls on his collar. He was still a disciple to a certain code of dress including his beloved 'Ben Sherman' and 'Sta Prest'. His boots had been swapped for the more foot, not to mention head, friendly tan loafer. He loved those tassels. It was too warm to complete the look with his beloved 'Crombie' but he had put on an acceptable sleeveless 'Fair Isle' jumper. He knew the pain he had caused Mary over the last few months, but she was his only hope now and he didn't want her leaving him, certainly not with Will. He felt in his pocket to make sure it was there.

As he headed nearer to the meeting place, his own mind went into overdrive. Without Mary he was a complete nothing, he thought. He always had his music and his dance of course into which he could escape. His devoted mother, Jenny, had become friendlier with Mrs Ashby, for whom she cleaned a few times a week. Mrs Ashby was heavily involved in the local church and Jenny had gone along with her. She had gained a new purpose in her life through God and spent a lot of time at the church these days. The upside of this was that she saw less of her husband, but the downside would be less contact with Jake who, despite all his faults, was still her son. His dad had been interviewed twice recently by the local constabulary about a spate of break-ins. He had been advised to ask for a series of other offences, including one of harassment, to be taken into account and was expecting a custodial sentence once it came to court. Joe had had a good run and he'd be well looked after inside!

Jake's other mates had left him for a better life with one of 'Her majesty's Forces'. Fergie was going soon on another tour of duty to Northern Ireland and although Drip had returned home, it was in a Union Jack covered box.

Jake would be completely on his own. He was really scared for the first time in his life. His anger brewed as he approached the meeting place.

The wasp landed gently on their joined hands and disturbed them from their individual thoughts. It momentarily caused Mary's hand to jerk gently.

'Vespula germanica,' authoritatively declared Will. 'Don't move' he continued, 'There's nothing here it needs so it will just fly away in a minute'.

As if on cue the wasp dutifully departed from their unmoved hands and Mary sighed a breath of relief.

The brief interruption allowed Will to formulate his bubbling question.

'Will you come to Spain with me for a couple of week's holiday?' he gushed out of his confused head without a stutter. All that previous worry, thought and construction finally composed into thirteen easy words: to which there were only two possible answers!

'I don't have a passport,' was the immediate alternative reply from a stunned Mary. Will looked at her and laughed. Only Mary could come up with that.

'Can I take that as a yes?', countered Will. The change of tack by him had taken her by complete surprise and unlike previous requests by Will to join him on his 'dream' there didn't seem any reason why not.

'Yes,' she said, making a selfish decision for the first time in her life. Will felt elated and pulled her to him and kissed her more passionately than ever before. Mary in turn reciprocated with equal passion.

The couple came into Jake's view at that moment and now his anger developed into a rage. He gripped the wood handle in his pocket and picked up speed in his journey toward the two, oblivious lovers. At fifty feet away, he removed the wood handle from his pocket, he pushed the handle's button and the spring immediately released the four-inch, shiny blade which glistened brightly in the summer sun.

'If I can't have her, then no one else can' he said to himself as he went into a sprint toward them at the edge of the 'Ravine'.

The heavy scrunch of rubble behind alerted them to the impending, uninvited arrival. They broke their clinch and quickly shuffled apart along the edge. They simultaneously looked into Jake's enraged features, his eyes red with anger with an incomprehensible sound emanating from his mouth.

He raised the knife above his head and angled it toward Mary. She screamed as Will attempted to rise from his seated position. Before Will could get to his feet and Mary had finished screaming one of Jake's tan loafers caught a protruding rock and he was catapulted over the edge and down the slope of the ravine with the knife tumbling before him. His size made sure he travelled quickly through the Harebell, Mugwort and Buckwheat down to the bottom. The names of the flowers perversely came back to Mary in that moment.

Jake hit the bottom with a severe crack as his 'suede head' hit a sharp rock.

Time stood still as Will and Mary tried to take in what had happened. They held each other and gasped as the viscous red liquid slowly oozed from Jake's broken skull. His previously white 'Ben' now matched the colour of his socks.

As they peered down, a 'Red Admiral' appeared from

nowhere and circled around Jake's deformed head. It found nothing of any interest there. It silently and majestically fluttered to the other end of his lifeless body and found solace on the tassel of his scuffed, tan loafer. It collapsed its two wings together to form a single sail and rested in peace with Jake.

Will and Mary stood together at the top of the slope, each with their private thoughts: Will knew then it would take time, but he was on the threshold of his ultimate dream. Mary knew then that the prison door was finally open. She was free at last.

Authors Note

Please consider giving feedback on this book.

Feedback is the lifeblood of writers.

It gives you the reader a chance to tell us just how good,
or bad we are.

If we offend, then please tell us.

If we entertain you, then please tell us
and others.

Printed in Great Britain
by Amazon